# Shooting for the Moon

Michael Kerry White

Copyright © 2015 Michael Kerry White

Second edition 2021

All rights reserved, including the right to reproduce this book, or portions thereof in any form. No part of this text may be reproduced, transmitted, downloaded, decompiled, reverse engineered, or stored, in any form or introduced into any information storage and retrieval system, in any form or by any means, whether electronic or mechanical without the express written permission of the author.

This is a work of fiction. Names and characters are the product of the author's imagination and any resemblance to actual persons, living or dead, is entirely coincidental.

The views expressed in this work are solely those of the author and do not necessarily reflect the views of the publisher, and the publisher hereby disclaims any responsibility for them.

ISBN: 9798517860224

PublishNation
www.publishnation.co.uk

## Note from the author:

I always wanted to own a blues bar but soon realised that I had neither the money, or the know how, to do so. Instead, I decided to write about one. Who knows, someone may want to make a film of it with loads of live blues music. Stranger things have happened.

*Shooting for the Moon* is a work of fiction and although I can relate to all the characters, I'm pretty sure none of it actually happened. However, if any character sounds like you then please take it as a compliment.

I also fully stand by the contention made in the book that most blues and rock musicians are slightly mad and I can provide a long list of names and incidents to prove this.

I hope you enjoy the book.

Michael Kerry White - 2021

Contact : shootingforthemoon@outlook.com

# Intro

If you're searching for insightful thoughts forget Socrates, (the old Greek philosopher guy not the old Brazilian footballer guy) and look no further than the lyrics of most blues songs. Take this as an example "Nobody loves me but my mother and she could be foolin' too." I think many of us can relate to that one. Some of the world's most enlightening quotes are right there in the lyrics.

For instance, Joseph Black (known to his friends, family and anyone else who knows him as Joby) often quotes bluesman Albert King, who wrote "If it weren't for bad luck, I wouldn't have no luck at all." Very apt. Since Joby was young the music in his head had provided a rolling soundtrack to his day reflecting the rhythms and places of his life. It would be mostly blues, Joby loves the blues but sometimes on a good day Stax soul (apparently Motown is too cheesy with all those violins and stuff). A hint of Wilson here maybe a touch of Otis there just helping him tick along. Most of his mates pass the time playing mental would I or wouldn't I games, while waiting for a bus or walking to the Job Centre, but not our Joby. Currently trolling round his brain is "Nobody loves you when you're down and out." He is not a happy soul these days.

It's a damp Tuesday morning in February and here he stands, staring bleakly into the bedroom mirror working on his tie, music rambling round his head. Joby Black, resident of the salubrious metropolis of High Wycombe, a once quaint market town in The Chilterns and now home to its own Islamic terrorists and The Eden Centre shopping experience. There is a local argument about which has done more damage. High Wycombe twinned with Islamabad and House of Frazer.

Wan sunlight permeates the drizzle and creeps through the net curtains as Joby stares on, brow furrowed, mouth set in a petulant pout, retying his tie once more. He sees himself as disenfranchised, an overwhelmingly oppressed minority. Middle aged, male, married and out of work again. Fortyfour years old and peering into the abyss of the long-term unemployment pooper.

It wasn't always like this. In his younger days he'd been seen as a bit of a lad. Considered then, by certain ladies of the town, to be ruggedly good looking. Time has now matured him into an average man of average height and average looks, his dark hair flecked with a hint of grey. Distinguished, Donna says. He counts himself fortunate to be married to the ethereal Donna but then again, seriously unfortunate on just about everything else in his world. He has lived in this same house all his life, a two up two down Victorian terrace which, in Estate Agent's jargon is nicely placed for town and station, excellent train links to Marylebone, a manageable sized garden and ideal for modernisation. A house that from the outside is plain, neat and tidy but once inside, reveals a house decked with an impressive array of crystals, wind chimes and dream catchers, all placed at strategic and sometimes totally inconvenient positions. This is because Donna is into new age, ambience and the mystical east. A Buddha for every occasion. Joby did once put forward an argument about "All this shite." but Donna just smiled her enigmatic smile and basically took no notice of him. That does seem to happen a lot.

Joby's Mum Sally died when he was eight, so for most his formative years it was just him and his dad, Tom. Well, Joby, Tom and when he was about Tom's brother, Ken. Tom had worked in the local furniture factories all his life whilst Ken seemingly didn't work anywhere, he just used to kip on the sofa, immune to comment and discomfort. He would just slump there with his legs hanging over the arm of the G-Plan. Said he'd slept in worse places. Maybe the copious alcohol helped deaden the pain. Being only eight years older than Joby, Ken was seen as more of a big brother than an uncle, plus he had the added kudos of being Wycombe's local rock guitar god. If anyone was going to make it, it'd be him (his words). Ken was the archetypical rocker, all hair and codpiece. Fall into The Nag's Head most weekends and there he would be with one of his bands, bursting the eardrums of many an unkempt, pimply youth. Ken was handsome though, in a strange hairy way and as sexually rampant as a dog with two dicks. Men liked Ken. Women _really_ liked Ken.

When Joby was growing up the house was always filled with music, fun and strange people. Blues and soul came from Tom's huge collection of tapes, 78's and 45's with exotic names from the past such as Son House, Leadbelly or Howlin' Wolf, coupled with strange tales of how Robert Johnson would practice in graveyards at night and then sell his soul to the devil at the Crossroads in exchange for the ability to play the guitar. Joby always wondered where those magic mystical crossroads were. The music and stories were his escape to a more exotic life. Meanwhile the rock, loud and heavy came from Ken. Musicians smelling of beer and leather were always in and out of the house, dossing on the floor or practising in the front room. In musical preferences, Joby definitely came down more on the side of the blues and soul, much cleaner, less whiffy, more mysterious. Songs telling of life in the deep south and American cities that Joby could only dream about visiting. Ken meanwhile, would hold court talking of life on the road with his various bands, relating the jolly japes he'd got up to in such glamorous places as Gateshead or Wrexham, though it was rumoured he did once go to Ostend on the ferry for the jazz festival. His favourite saying was "You should always shoot for the moon" usually as a lead up to some hugely outlandish scheme that would invariably fall on its arse, but that would have Joby laughing at the front and balls of it all. The hackneyed term was loveable rogue but indeed that's what he was. Life was simple and life was fun.

That all suddenly changed when just after Joby's $20^{th}$ birthday Tom died of liver failure. There were no warnings, just gone in a weekend, a huge void appearing in Joby's life. Joby took the step from youth to adult in three days. A year or so after that, Ken went away again but this time for good. Nobody knew where he'd gone, not many people seemed surprised or cared and although Joby initially tried half heartedly to find him, everyday life took over and after a while Ken slipped into memory. Joby always looked back on those days with great affection but also tinged with regret at how it was taken away from him and how, as an ageing orphan of 21, he was left to fend for himself. Not a word from Ken for 20 odd years, sweet sod all, nothing, nada, zip. That was until two weeks ago when out of the blue the hairy codpiece did indeed turn up, in a manner of speaking.

# Chapter 1

Joby stares deeply into the bedroom mirror, forlornly looking for life on the other side and not finding any. An incredibly grumpy face stares back as he struggles with the intricacies of the Windsor knot. Bad enough when you're working but surely one of the benefits of being a dosser is not having to wear a tie, let alone a suit. There must be some hidden bonus to mid-life unemployment, surely.

He sticks his head around the bedroom door and pathetically calls out hoping for a last-minute reprieve "Why do I have to wear a tie?"

From downstairs comes an indistinct reply but the tone carried the message of noncompromise. He tries again "I still don't understand your logic! "

Donna's ethereal voice carries up the stairs, her tone as if she is talking to a petulant teenager. "Well, like I told you, several times, it's out of respect for your Uncle Ken. You need to look tidy... for a change. You are his only living relative don't forget."

Joby retreats and flumps about the bedroom grumbling, looking for matching shoes. After an unsuccessful foray under the bed, he finds them stashed in the back of the wardrobe. Footware located he grabs his only suit jacket, holds it up, peers at it, warily sniffs it and tries, in vain, to scratch some indeterminate stain off of the collar. He mumbles on "Ken never owned a suit in his life. Used to call men in suits spivs. I never, ever saw him in a suit" He knows Donna is right though. As usual.

A last look in the mirror, a last sigh and he slowly descends to find said Donna in the kitchen tapping something into her phone. Tuesday is Donna's tai chi morning and so there she is resplendent in a black cotton Chinese number looking cool and collected. A picture of ethereal calm, unlike her husband who is miserable and well, flumpy.

*FLUMPY – adjective (1) the propensity to set (something or oneself) down with or as if with a noise. (2) Joby Black.*

If Donna is the ying then Joby most definitely is the yang. She finishes her typing "There just popped a tweet on Twitter. I've got 82 followers now."

"Why do you bother with all that shite? Who cares if Simon Cowell's dog has had a dump."

"Well, it keeps me connected."

She looks him up and down, scratches at his lapel, adjusts his tie then with an approving nod "That's better."

Joby just stands dejectedly, hands hanging at his sides, shoulders slumped. The aura of the beaten man pervading from him. One last vain attempt "Donna, I still have no idea why I'm dressed up. It's just the solicitors."

Donna steps forward and puts her hands on his shoulders. Her head tilted, dark hair hanging across one side of her face, she fixes her hazel eyes lovingly on his, a sympathetic smile playing on her lips. She is indeed poised in the sympathise position. Many men will know and still be fooled by this pose. Then in the time-honoured fashion that wives have in dealing with whining husbands she totally changes the subject.

"Now you're sure you're ok going on your own today. It's the last Tai Chi class and I wouldn't want to miss it. We're doing White Crane."

Joby drops (flumps) on to a kitchen chair feigning interest "White Crane? Fascinating. Does it involve standing on one leg and sticking your head up your arris. I'd pay good money to see that?"

"No, it doesn't. It's very therapeutic, you should try it."

"Should I? Should I really? I have enough trouble standing on two legs these days let alone one. Another time maybe."

Another big sigh and a glum shake of the head. "You know what gets me? Twenty odd years and not a word from the old sod and now, true to his belligerent awkward self, he's snuffed it. Nah you'll be alright Donna, Digger's volunteered to come with me. We won't be there that long I shouldn't think."

Donna delicately sits on his lap and this time she really does sympathise. "Look, I know it's sad but anything you get will be a nice memento wont it."

"Suppose so. As long as it isn't any of his old t-shirts or boxers or something similarly disgusting. I think I still got some in the rag box in the garage."

He glances out of the window and sees a figure bouncing up the path "Ah here's the boy now."

Donna jumps up and opens the back door for Digger to breeze in. Now Joby has lots of acquaintances but Digger is his best friend, some would say maybe his only real friend. The pair go back a long way to college days where they had struck up a friendship during a Gino Washington gig. Digger Jones is a surprise package. Slim, blonde (well blondish/grey these days) Digger had been a bass player in a few bands that had nearly made it in days gone by but had forsaken his quest for fame and fortune after he'd met Pandora. For the past fifteen years he and his wife had run a particularly profitable surgical implant business, supplying plastic surgeons with the bits and bobs necessary to fill copious bras and thereby, fulfil many a male fantasy. Had, being the operative word as they recently sold up and now owned a very nice bank balance instead. Digger, as is his style, was in an old blue jacket, t-shirt, jeans and Converse trainers. Ageing rocker chic.

Joby looked down at his own uncomfortable outfit and then at his friend's.

"Well, this is a first. I never thought I'd be jealous of your dress sense Digger but today, what can I say."

Digger strikes a pose "Say nothing young man but simply feast your eyes. It's a fashion statement."

"Really? And what statement is that. Shop at Oxfam? Is that piss and talc I can smell?"

Digger twirls around "Well you've got it or you haven't and apparently I have. Oh, sorry I'm late by the way, popped into the shops." He wryly surveys Joby's attire "Is that a new tie?"

"Yes, very funny, you're bleeding hilarious you are. What did you buy? Anything decent?"

"A hammock, in Wilkinsons. Ten quid, bargain."

Joby doesn't want to but knows he is going to have to ask "A hammock? Why may I ask? "

Digger picks up Joby's battered briefcase and hands it to him "Never had one always wanted one. Need something to laze in when Pandora and I shift to warmer climes."

Joby heads for the door "Oh yes, the big move, I forgot."

Donna enquires after Mrs. Jones "And how is Pandora? All packed for the weekend? I really must start thinking about what to take. Is it cold in Amsterdam Digger?"

"Much like here I think Donna." He eases past Joby at the door, stops and turns "Packed? Oh yeah, her case is stuffed already. I'll just shove some things in a carrier bag. She's really excited though about going back to where we had our first encounter, if you know what I mean. A sort of pilgrimage."

Joby guides him out through the back door with a helping hand on his shoulder.

"Sounds lovely, I know I can't wait. Is there one of those blue plaques on the wall? Digger Jones pulled here." He stops for a final check in his briefcase "Still I suppose it'll be a break of sorts. Though having said that I don't know how much of a break with you and that mad Dutch woman."

He blows Donna a kiss and heads out "See you later Donna. Enjoy your Shiatsu"

"Tai chi you joker."

Joby calls back "Yeah I knew that. If we're late you'll know where to find us. At the charity shop donating Ken's pants."

\* \* \*

The pair amble down the front path to Digger's car and climb in. Joby is unusually quiet, inside his head though the blues are twanging away.

"You ok Joby?"

Joby considers the question "You know what Dig, I'm really so angry at him. Pissing off like that and then …. dying. What a selfish bastard."

Digger chuckles "Indeed, how selfish can a person be dying and not consulting you? Well, no point worrying about it now, it's happened and you need to get on with your life." He starts the car.

Joby slowly turns to stare at his friend, a bemused look drifts across his face like a cloud over the moon as he considers Digger's statement "Get .. on .. with .. my .. life? Some fucking life! Alright for you moneybags."

They pull away and Joby stares out of the window. "Further on down the road." rolls around his head.

*You got to reap just what you sow,*
*that old saying is true*
*You got to reap just what you sow,*
*that old saying is true*
*Like you mistreat someone,*
*someone's gonna mistreat you*

\* \* \*

Lost in thought Joby watches the shops and offices of Easton Street drift past. Next to him Digger burbles on but Joby only takes in snippets of random chatter and chirruping.

"….. and it smelled of fish. I said to her I won't be going down there again believe me."

Joby suddenly lets out a yelp and an exclamation as he swivels in his seat and stares out of the window. A pink frontage slips past.

"What the fu..? What have they done to The Nags Head? It's pink with a big rainbow on the front!!! Digger?"

"Oh yeah it's under new management. Called The Pride now."

Joby stares out through the windscreen a totally bewildered look on his face. His friend might as well be talking Swahili.

"The Pride? Did you say ... The Pride?" He processes the information "What sort of stupid name is that? What's wrong with The Nags Head. Perfectly good name. A historical name, in fact going back to the time of, oh who knows whenever .... Pink? For fuck's sake what is this town coming to."

"It's a gay pub."

Joby turns in his seat and stares at Digger. "A Gay pub? What, The Nags Head? A gay pub? What are you trying to tell me Digger?"

Digger is exasperated at Joby's seemingly lack of comprehension "Bloody hell Joby it's not that hard. The Nags Head is now called The Pride and The Pride is a gay pub. Sign of the times."

Joby stares on pondering this additional unwanted change to his existence. He makes a proclamation.

"Digger, kill me now. Frankly I don't care if it's gay, straight or slightly askew but if that's a sign of the times just get me the rubber hose and close the garage doors." He ponders some more "I can't believe it. All those crap bands we used to see there, the overpowering smell of leather, the overflowing urinals, the obligatory punch ups. I mean where can you go now to get that sort of entertainment?"

Digger thinks for a second "Nowhere round here mate."

As his adolescense disappears in a flash of pink Joby lets out a huge sigh of disappointment and slumps further into the seat, his suit collar riding up making him look like a disenchanted gremlin," End of an era Dig. End of an era."

He stares some more and then thinks about Digger's earlier ramblings "So you didn't like the Sushi bar then?"

They continue along the London Road in silence, the soundtrack in Joby's head morphing to some slow bottleneck guitar blues. Life was shit and rapidly getting shittier. After a further five minutes or so the car turns into a small car park at the back of an old Georgian house and Digger manoeuvres into a tight parking space. He leaps out with enthusiasm.

"Come on Joby lets go and see what Ken's left you."

Joby slowly climbs out and follows him grudgingly across the cobbled car park. They push through the heavy doors and Joby trudges up to the reception desk, pulling a letter from his old briefcase as he goes.

An attractive young lady sitting behind the desk looks up from her magazine "May I help you?"

"Joby Black to see." He looks down at the letter "Mr. Williams."

"Take a seat Mr. Black. I'll tell Mr. Williams you are here."

He joins Digger on the circa 1970 black, leatherette settee. An unloved rubber plant is standing in a tub filled with what appears to be hundreds of rabbit droppings or dry roasted peanuts. Its forlorn leaves hang over the chrome arms of the sofa making it a tight fit for the two of them. The obligatory glass coffee table is strewn with a selection of old magazines. Digger stares at the receptionist as Joby grabs a tattered Readers Digest and flicks through the pages.

"Well I never, Harold Wilson's dead." He continues to browse "Oh look - Twenty things to do with a Cucumber." He nudges Digger "Twentyone if you eat it I guess."

Digger's focus remains on the receptionist. She looks up as he gives her his best boyish smile. Joby glances at his friend with amusement.

"You'll have no luck there, mate."

"Just being polite." He sits back "You know, I depped in a band with your Uncle Ken once. He was very good. Out of his head most of the time of course, but surprisingly good."

Joby throws the magazine back on the pile "No wonder I grew up deranged and confused then."

He considers his past "You know my Mum and Dad always wanted me to get into music, so they bought an old piano. It was a big thing with both of them. Practice your scales they used to nag. You'll always get invited to parties if you can play the piano they said. Guess what? Didn't get invited to one. Ken got invited to loads. Scales were the only finger exercise I got as a teenager."

He turns to Digger "Now I come think about it I guess old Ken must have had some influence on me."

It's Digger's turn to be surprised "Old Ken? He was only what, seven, eight years older than you? Must have been nice having someone more mature looking out for you."

Joby slowly turns and stares at Digger nonplussed at his friend's notion "Mature? We're talking about Ken here remember. I don't know who looked after who most of the time. He was like one of those mutts from the dog rescue out at Stokenchurch. Oh, a great novelty at first but a pain when they've crapped on your best Axminster a few times. And then of course you're too embarrassed to take them back, so you're stuck with the little shitzus."

Digger reminisces "We had a rescue dog, bearded collie, Rufus. Peed on Pandora's wedding dress. Three times as I recall. I loved that dog."

Joby folds his arms "I know Ken was a bit of a waster, and a complete liability, but it would have been nice to have seen him again. Now, too late."

A sad silence descends on them. Digger resumes his totty watch.

The receptionist's phone buzzes. "Yes Mr. Williams. Certainly." She leans over the counter giving Digger a brief flash of cleavage. "Mr. Williams will see you now Mr. Black. It's the door in the far corner."

"Thank you. Digger, close your mouth, let's get this over with."

They cross the reception area and knock on the appointed door. It's opened by an older man with short grey hair, a grey suit, grey shoes and glasses. This man has never seen a colour chart. He shakes hands and ushers them in to seats by a large desk that is cluttered with buff files and papers. The Grey Man takes his place behind it.

"Thank you for coming Mr. Black my name is David Williams. Please take a seat." He looks Digger up and down "And may I ask who you are?"

Joby quickly interjects "Ah, this is Mr. Digby Jones, an acquaintance of my Uncle Ken and though I hate to admit it, my oldest and most trusted friend. Mr. Jones is here to kindly support me in my time of loss and to drive me home, as my wife has the car this morning and is, at this precise moment, in all probability, stood on one leg imitating a large aquatic bird."

The solicitor coughs somewhat taken aback and quickly picks up a file from a stack in front of him.

He addresses Joby "Shall we get down to business? Now did you bring the means of identification I requested?"

Joby reaches into his briefcase and pulls out his passport and birth certificate and passes them across the desk "I certainly did. Took some finding I can tell you."

Tapping his birth certificate, he turns to Digger "See, proof I'm not what you've been calling me all these years."

Digger shakes his head "Proves nothing mate. They can be forged you know."

Mr. Williams interjects impatiently. "Mr. Black if we can start?"

"Oh right, of course and please call me Joby everyone does."

Seeing Mr. Williams' questioning expression he added "Joseph Black, Joe B, Joby "

"If you insist Mr. Bl...Joby. So, as you will be well aware your uncle lived what I can only call, an unusual life. His lifestyle was not what you could call in any sense, everyday."

A smile crosses Joby's face as he remembers Ken "Lucky old sod I say Mr. Williams."

"Um maybe. And as you are aware, he left these shores some twenty years ago."

"Really? No idea where he went, just know he went."

"Well, it transpires that he joined what I believe is called, in musical parlance, a death thrash metal band in the United States and played with them up until his untimely demise last month in a Las Vegas hot tub. And Las Vegas is where he is now buried. Plot 1047 east, The Woodlawn Cemetery, 1500 Las Vegas Blvd North to be precise."

The two stare at him in a mixture of disbelief and incredulity.

Mr. Williams continues "Although the exact details of his passing are still somewhat hazy, it seems that he died naked in the company of what I believe the Americans term um…a hooker. A young Mexican lady named Mel-on-ie."

He peers over his glasses "According to the aforementioned, Mel-on-ie, his last recorded words were, ahem." He affects a serious tone "Hit it one more time. At which point he apparently slumped forward and floated face down in the hot tub until the paramedics arrived and pronounced him dead."

The office suddenly seems claustrophobic as Joby sits in the stunned silence composing himself. "Umm oh right…. Ah … well … Still, I can think of worse ways to go Mr. Williams. Proud to hear he was holding up the Black name. Well holding up something at least."

"Quite.It also seems prior to his demise he amazingly made a great deal of money. Apparently, his band, Cocky Magpie, had a massive cult following there and over the years he amassed a considerable fortune."

The incredulity continues as Joby and Digger sit open mouthed like fledgling cuckoos.

Mr. Williams continues, "I have to inform you though, that he also managed to spend most of it. He gambled, drank and had numerous expensive liaisons. However, the residue of his estate he has left entirely to you Mr. Black :… Joby."

He points behind them to a small table sat against the far wall. On it sits a brown manila envelope, a badly charred electric guitar, of indecernible colour, that had seen much better days and a set of keys. Joby stares until Digger chips in.

"Ooh a Fender Stratocaster, that would have been great in it's day."

Joby is still staring at the table "Is that it? Keys, an envelope and that thing?"

"Yes. The keys are for your uncle's workshop which it seems still has some considerable time remaining on its lease. I understand he had certain plans for it but never had the chance to realise them. The envelope contains a letter for you and some magazine clippings. The guitar by the way, despite it's condition, was your Uncle's pride and joy."

Joby lets out a snort "Pride and joy? Looks a pile of ......" Sighing Joby slumps back "Brilliant. Un-sodding-believable. Twenty years of nothing and now a bolloxed guitar, some cuttings from Kerrang and a lock up. Any pants? No? I'd have rather had the pants."

"None I'm afraid. Just what you see there."

Mr. Williams slowly walks to the table and picks up the manila envelope and hands it to a dazed Joby.

Digger however, is enthused by it all "Open it Jobes.See what it says." Joby slowly pulls out a wad of magazine cuttings which he throws on the desk and a letter which he starts to read.

"Ok. It says." He begins to scan "Dear Joby, If you are reading this then I have gone to that great gig in the sky. Blah blah blah. - Da da da can't take it with you but I never intended to… blah blah amazed I have anything left. The doctors said I had to give up wine, women and song and not being much of a singer I decided that one out of three was a good compromise. What's left I leave to you. Blah blah no children and you the only family I have. I hope you've been shooting for the moon and that the Black genes are alive and kicking. - Yep, unfortunately they are Kenny boy." He turns the page and continues "Big plans which I never got to put into place, success late in life, want you to find some too. Blah blah initiate something that will carry on my musical heritage. – Musical heritage? What musical heritage, he's bleeding deluded. - Solicitor has instructions to pay you the sum of £100,000 cash- Ah now that's more like it - However this will only be handed over when you devise and present a suitable and acceptable plan for this heritage project. - Unbelievable! What a knob! I hope that you remember me fondly… Not now you dick no. The plan must be presented to Mr. Williams who, as my trusted executor, will then decide whether it's a goer or not. I also leave you my treasured guitar and the keys to my lockup. - Treasured, he couldn't even look after that. Thanks a bunch Kenny boy." He finishes the letter "Use them wisely Joby. Rock on. Kenton Black"

Joby sits upright pondering his legacy as Digger picks up the letter and silently rereads it.

Joby sighs a perplexed sigh "A hundred grand, brilliant but music heritage? What's he want, a Kenton Black Death Metal Museum?" His face takes on a bemused stare "Where do I start? I mean don't get me wrong, I love music but…" He wriggles in his seat "And a lock up. Why would he keep a lock up? What the hell am I supposed to do with it?"

Heavy silence reigns in the solicitor's office until Joby lets out an even bigger resigned sigh.

"I suppose I'd better go and have a butchers at the place. Plus of course, let's not forget the piece de resistance, one knackered guitar. Christmas come early wouldn't you say."

Mr. Williams is all business "Mr. Black your uncle was very specific about the handing over of the money. When do you think you can come back to me? No plan no money you understand."

"Well, we're off to Holland on Friday for the weekend so, some time after that I guess." He shrugs his shoulders "Is that it then? Any more surprises?"

"None. Indeed Mr. Black that is all. Have an enjoyable trip and I look forward to seeing you on your return. If you have any questions, please feel free to call me."

He stands indicating the meeting is over and extends his hand. They all shake hands and Joby puts the keys, documents and cuttings into his old briefcase.

"Well thanks for everything, I think." He slowly heads for the door but Mr. Williams calls after him. Joby turns to see him holding the guitar.

"Mr. Bl....Joby, haven't you forgotten something?

Joby trudges back and takes it from him "Ah yes. Silly me, thanks a lot."

\* \* \*

Digger smiles a goodbye to the receptionist and jogs to catch up a despondent Joby who is tramping across the dank car park. The drizzle reflects his grey mood and, in his head, some mournful blues whine. Digger unlocks the car and then holds the boot open for Joby to drop the guitar in. Not a word is said as he climbs in the passenger seat and Digger sets off for home.

As they near the town Joby suddenly blurts out "What a wanker!" Silence descends once more.

*Was a time when you'd be here by my side*
*Oh, but the rain came down*
*Washed it all away*
*Now I stand alone with my guitar and play*

\* \* \*

They park outside Joby's house and troop back up the path and into the kitchen. It's warm and welcoming. Donna has returned and is upstairs singing some tuneless show song. Digger makes himself comfortable at the kitchen table whilst Joby heads outside, carrying the guitar under his arm. After a couple of minutes, he returns empty handed.

"There. That's that in the shed out the way. Pride and joy, pah."

But Digger is in an optimistic mood "Hey, it might come in useful. I could probably do something with it."

Joby sits down opposite him "Digger, I could do something with it too but bonfire night's months away."

He passes Digger the magazine cuttings "You might as well have these for your collection though."

"Cheer's mate. Much appreciated."

"I had a quick glance but nothing really interesting. Just a couple of paragraphs about Ken in his thrashing heyday that I've kept. Stick the rest in your scrapbook."

Donna floats into the kitchen "Hello boys. So how did it go? Are we millionaires by any chance, can we retire to a life of luxury?"

Joby gently takes her hand and guides her to sit on his lap "I need to break this to you gently. No."

Donna is sympathetic "Well never mind, chins up. What did they say?"

Joby relates the mornings proceedings and explains "So we are now the proud owners of a lock up, somewhere down by the railway, a piece of burnt timber that was once a guitar, bits of old magazines and the task of finding a suitable £100,000 musical memorial for good old Kenton Black. I think I can safely say I've had more sane mornings Donna believe me."

Donna takes his face in her hands and kisses his forehead "Baby it's a challenge. I'm sure you will come up with something. You're nothing if not inventive darling. Have you seen the lockup yet? Now that could be handy."

Joby shakes his head "Really? Handy for what? Nah we came straight home. I'll pop down tomorrow, if I have time. Anyway, back to the real world, how was your origami?"

Donna smiles knowing he is teasing. She loves Joby teasing her "Tai chi!"

Joby smiles "Yeah I knew that."

"And it was great, thank you very much."

Donna jumps up and performs a selection of Tai Chi poses in front of them "You Philistines. Tai Chi is a Chinese system of physical exercises designed especially for meditation and self-defence. So, watch out."

"Well, if we ever need a slow motion Ninja I know where to come."

Digger stands up "Hey I'm off, see you both Friday. We'll pick you up around seven thirty, ok? Pandora will be up around four getting dolled up so I'll get her to give you a buzz."

Joby goes over to him and pats him fondly on the back "Ok Diggs and thanks for this morning. Who knows maybe Ken will send us a message from below, give us a clue or something?" Then as an afterthought "Will you be bringing the hammock?"

Digger chuckles as he heads out "If you want. See you Friday. Did I say nice suit by the way?" He trots down the path before Joby can retort.

Donna puts a comforting arm around his shoulders as he closes the door "Was it sad?"

Joby thinks and frowns "Yeah a little. You know I really missed him at first and now, he's gone for good. I'm as much angry at him as upset."

"Listen this could be an opportunity for you, for us. You know I believe things happen for a reason so let's just go with it eh? It'll be an adventure. "

Joby shrugs "Ok. Though can I still be angry with him for a while. Please."

"Ok just for a minute or two."

She stands up and takes Joby's hand "Come on my little soldier. I'll do some Reiki on you, soothe away those troubles. Then we must get on and do some packing."

Joby smiles rubbing his hands together "Day's looking up already. You will be gentle with me won't you?"

As he climbed the stairs his soundtrack was much more up tempo.

*Once it come along a dime by the dozen*
*That ain't nothin' but ten cent lovin'*
*Hey little thing, let me light your candle*
*'Cause mama I'm sure hard to handle, now, gets around*

# Chapter 2

Amsterdam has two physical states, charming or skanky. There seemingly is no in between. The canals, though picturesque, are full of graphite coloured water littered with strange flotsam and jetsam and the local population all appear to worship at the church of piercings and tattoos. On this particular Saturday lunch time it was charming with skanky periods.

So far, the friends had done Anne Frank, the Rijksmuseum and the flower market and now as a special treat Donna and Pandora have hit the shops leaving the boys sat in the Bayou Street Blues Bar just off Leidseplein. Pandora could be described as statuesque, or as Joby once said "Able to kill a man, given enough time" and was prone to wearing skin tight leather trousers (as she is today) and anything that showed off her ample bosom. She had kidnapped Digger some 20 years earlier right here in Amsterdam. In fact, at the same Bayou Street Blues Bar, when he was playing with a Deep Purple tribute band and she was out on the town. Pandora had decided that night that Digger was the one. He would, basically, have no say in it and furthermore that his life as a struggling musician wasn't going to fund her future. They'd fallen for each other instantly and had over the past years started and sold a very lucrative enhancement business. Pandora now was taking on the immense challenge of spending as much of the company proceeds as she could before Digger discovered his balls and stopped her.

So, whilst the girls caused plastic carnage in the neighbouring shops, Digger and Joby sat enjoying a local beer and watching a lunchtime band do musical damage to Delbert McClinton and Robben Ford. The Bayou Street Blues Bar is at the far end of Leidsekruisstraat, a small cobbled street just off the Leidseplein. The narrow street is lined with restaurants and from the outside it looks like any bar in Amsterdam. Inside, it was as basic as it could be. A wooden floor stained from years of abuse, a narrow shelf for standing glasses on running down the left-hand wall, the bar on the right backed by ornate flemish mirrors and a compact stage at the rear next to the solitary toilet. A few small tables for tourists to sit at are dotted about but locals just stand at the bar drinking and talking. It was almost exactly what a blues bar should be, nothing fancy but somewhere to meet and listen to music. It certainly wouldn't win any prizes for décor or indeed plaudits from the health and safety people.

Digger had been talking non-stop about how he had first met Pandora but Joby had switched off some ten minutes earlier, lost in his own thoughts. Just sitting and staring into the distance. The band played on.

"So, this is where it happened. Just over there by the bar. I was here playing with The….." He's talking to himself as Joby interrupts excitedly.

"Digger this is it. Listen, I think this is what the old sod meant. His musical heritage. Well not this, but something similar. Less ….. less shitty."

Digger looks about, not understanding what on earth his friend is referring to.

"Listen brain of Britain, I had a quick look at that lock up before we came away and it's a good size, and not a bad location."

Digger is still puzzled, "And? So?"

"And. So, my little friend, what better way to immortalise Ken's wonderful contribution to the burgeoning death thrash metal scene, than to, yes, you've guessed it."

He holds his hands out waiting for the penny to drop. In the end he gives in "Correct, open a blues bar."

Digger's mouth drops open and he is about to question the leap of logic.

But Joby pre-empts him. "What? Well, we're not opening a bloody heavy metal biker bar stinking of leather and piss. As you said, sign of the times. Listen if the Nags Head can go pink, we can go blue. If the ghost of Kenton Black doesn't like it, he can kiss my earthbound arse …. or haunt me…. which he probably will"

Digger sits back and takes a sip of his drink "Well it's an idea of sorts, I guess. But what do you know about running a blues bar?"

Joby sits forward his row furrowed, a puzzled look on his face "What do I know about running a blues bar? Are you mad? Absolutely sod all of course. But how hard can it be? See, I knew I would come up with another great idea. Donna was right. It's a talent."

It's Digger's turn to lean forward. He reaches across the table and puts his hand affectionately on Joby's forearm, as if about to explain a riddle to a small child.

"Joby, I need to break this to you gently. You don't have a talent or great ideas come to that. Donna humours you. In all the years I've known you, you've never had one great idea. Never had one good idea even, probably never will. It's a fact of life"

They both sit back. Joby is perplexed. So Digger presses on "Plenty of stupid ideas of course. Oh my, yes, loads of them. I could write a book about them"

Now Joby is affronted "What? Give me one example. Go on. "

Digger leans forward again "Ok. Remember our summer job in college."

"Yeah, what about it?"

"Well remember when you had us pose as estate agents, to attract women, cos women went for smoothies in suits according to you."

"That is a proven fact. What's ya point?"

Digger's voice rises as he remembers the humiliation "The point being, all our job actually was, was to bang in For Sale signs. You had me in a three-piece suit sweating like a pig all summer, while you posed about like a nonce. We'll be rolling in birds you said."

Joby can't see a problem here "We were rolling in birds."

"Really? Barely a sniff of any totty for me, apart from one who you promptly nicked. I lost a stone in weight and ruined my best Burton suit that year. I'm amazed I ever made any money after having you as a friend."

Joby shrugs this slight off as an obvious mistake "Ungrateful sod. I did ok, loads of crumpet. It was a great wheeze. Like I say, it's a talent."

Digger shakes his head and sips his drink "So I agree you have ideas but ninety-nine-point nine percent of the time they are, how can I put it, shit."

"High praise, thanks."

Digger isn't finished yet as he delivers the coup de grace "And talk me through that car valeting experience."

"A simple mixing error that's all. So, chemicals burn leather, who'd of guessed?"

"Well, anyone with an ounce of common sense basically."

Joby presents his case "Listen, firstly the instructions were unreadable. Printed in Czech. You were no help."

Digger sits open mouthed "You are amazing Joby. So now it's my fault."

Joby shrugs "Hey it was a painful experience Digger."

"Painful experience? Yes, especially for the poor sod from Gerrards Cross whose Merc you ruined and of course the other poor sod who helped foot the bill, namely me."

Joby is unfazed "I seem to recall you offered. Though as always Digger it was gratefully received."

"Yeah, well add it to that long, long bill." Another gulp of beer.

Joby ploughs on "Ok will do, but that's old history. I want to make new history. Trouble is Ken's £100k isn't really enough so I'm going to need to find a partner."

Feigning a defeated air, he slumps back in his seat and glances at his friend. Digger doesn't bite and carries on drinking. Joby baits the swim a bit more.

"But naturally, I can understand your reluctance in getting involved. Who can blame you with the big move coming up?"

Digger has a baffled look on his face "Er. I wasn't going to get involved thanks."

Joby takes the nonchalant approach "Nah, you know what, it wouldn't appeal to you anyway. Not really up your street. Bit of a risk. Possibly more for someone who has, oh I don't know, vision, drive and actually understands the music business."

Joby's mental bite alarm goes off as Digger snatches the bait "Now you're taking the piss. I have drive and vision. Pandora and I made a great success of our business and I know more about music than anyone around. Don't forget I had a hit record."

"Not sure number 37 in Portugal really counts Dig."

"27 actually and very big in Denmark as well. And tell me who was the first to realise the Lighthouse Family were crap. Eh? Think about that."

"Fair play, I'll grudgingly give you that one."

Joby looks around and leans towards his pal in a conspiratorial fashion, speaking in a low tone "OK if you insist here's the deal. Now, I know how hasty you can be so all I ask is that you don't dismiss it until you've thought about it. Run it up the flagpole and see if it flaps around, ok?"

He pauses for effect "We go 50/50. A hundred grand each, equal shares in the business."

The big fish that is Digger fights back "Are you mad? I don't have that sort of money to chuck away."

Joby throws his arms in the air "Right! Well, you gave that a good deal of consideration then. You're bleeding loaded you tight arse."

Digger is indignant "There's nothing to consider and I'm not loaded, just comfortable thank you."

"Ha! Comfortable! You made a fortune out of tits and bits." Another pause for effect "So the chance of being a name in the music business again, well I say again, doesn't appeal to you, does it?"

Digger shakes his head "Nope can't say it does."

Joby tries the emotional blackmail route "And of course a chance to work with your closest and dearest friend. I am hurt and saddened Digger."

Digger leans forward "You see, that's it, it's the dearest friend bit that really worries me."

Joby ignores the slight "Think about it logically. We both have spare cash."

He points at Digger "Vous, company sale." Points to himself "Mois, Kenny's money." He points back and forth "Kenny, sale, sale, Kenny."

Digger is losing patience "Yes I get the message. So, I have some cash, that doesn't mean I am going to blow it on your hare-brained scheme."

Joby tries Donna's tried and tested technique. He ignores Digger "Think. With that cash, we can have all this. No, I lie! A much better version of this, and also provide Ken his memorial thingy."

Suddenly he's serious "Imagine. Blues music to the great unwashed. And let's face it Digger most of your mates are well, greatly unwashed."

Digger thinks but can't argue with the last statement "Cruel, but true."

"Remember The Nags Head? Gone to be replaced by a puce gin palace with Tainted Love on the P.A."

Digger decides it's time to end this discussion with his closing argument "Joby it won't work and I'll tell you why. If you remember I did years off and on playing in cack clubs."

"Indeed you did, shit holes."

"Exactly. And I never saw one I would want to go back to, let alone spend money on. Life's been good since then and now I'm "retired", so to speak, and have a few bob. So, Pandora and I are going find a little place in the sun where I can laze, in my Wilkinsons hammock, and live La Vida loco. She deserves her husband's full attention. So, my cash is not, as you put it, spare."

Joby smiles a condescending smile at his friend.

"Ok. I hear what you are saying but Digger let me explain something."

He counts on his fingers "Firstly, every band you were in was cack so, of course, you played in cack clubs. Secondly, Pandora would probably, no, definitely kill you after three weeks of being alone with you. Hey, I want to kill you after half an hour and I'm your best friend. I tell you what, let's ask your boss when she gets back from spending all your dosh because, I know what she'll say."

Digger is dismissive "She will say what I just said, believe me. And she is not my boss. We have a joint arrangement."

Joby snorts "Of course you do. Digger trust me. I have seen the lockup and it would be perfect. No neighbours, well none that are living apart from the winos and a car repair place, plus good parking. This is our new start."

"I don't need a new start."

"Well fucking good for you! I do. Think about it at least."

They lapse into silence but curiosity finally gets the better of Digger "Ok where is this lock up?"

"Evergreen St. Under the viaduct where that old branch line used to run, three arches to be precise."

Digger's face wrinkles as if smelling something rancid "A very wholesome area, I don't think."

"It's not that bad. Apparently, Ken got it from the railway on a long lease, cheap. We'd just do it up minimal inside, wooden floor, bar, stage, posters and pictures on the wall. Maybe a few of your old guitars and that piece of junk his nibs left me nailed up. Couple of staff, couple of bogs, perfect."

Digger ponders. The band file back on stage ready to cause more musical bloodshed as Pandora and Donna totter in laden down with bags which they drop by the table.

Pandora towers over them. She enquires in her anglo/dutch accent "All right boys? Fantastisch out there." She peers into Digger's face "What you looking so ellendig about?

Joby leaps in "Alright girls?"

He looks in one of Pandora's bags "I see they have a Tarts R Us here then."

He then spys Donna's purchases and is less impressed "Donna not more crystals! For god's sake woman."

Donna smiles an ethereal smile and blows Joby a kiss. End of argument.

Joby turns his concentration elsewhere "Pandora, pull up those chairs, I have something to ask your opinion on."

The girls settle as Joby continues "Now which would you rather, own half of a blues bar with Donna and I or, vegetate and grow old in Spain with Sir Whinge-alot here."

Digger goes on the attack "Just say no to everything, it's a trick."

Joby ploughs on "We're considering opening a blues bar and Digger here wasn't sure what you'd say. Equal shares of course." He points at Digger's miserable face." He's very excited you can tell."

"I ain't and we aren't. I know what my beautiful Pandora will say." He pokes a finger at Joby "He's a deluded tosser."

Then trying to gain bonus points with Pandora "Ooh I like your new dress angel, very fetching."

She ignores him as she looks down her nose at Joby "A Blues Bar?" There follows a long pause, wheels whirring in her head, as she thinks it through "Fantastisch idea, why not, I'm musical. I was in the school choir, third place at the Rotterdam Zomer Carnaval. We sang Heer Halewijn."

She nods towards Digger "He needs shomething like that to get him out of the house. Sounds fun to me."

She ruffles Digger's hair "He is a miserable little Worst lately, moping around all day. Mr. Mopey I call him. We can't go out until Bargain Hunt finishes. No offence Digger."

Digger sighs and rearranges his mane "Oh none taken. Anyway Joby, we are not, I repeat not, opening a blues bar. No way, not at all. End of story. I have said my last word on this subject so lets just drop it and enjoy the rest of the weekend, shall we?"

Nobody is listening to him. Donna eyes Joby "And who's idea is this may I ask."

Joby defensively holds up his hands "Don't look at me. We both came up with it just Digs didnt know he'd thought of it. He would have of course, given enough time. But he has to take some of the credit."

Joby, ready to land his fish, is now talking solely to Pandora "Ken's lockup, well my lockup now, is ideal. It's under the viaduct down Evergreen Street, three arches."

Digger mumbles "It'll be a dump believe me."

"Now I'm sure this was the project he had in mind before he wandered off into the sunset. Obviously, fate brought us in here." He waves his arms around.

Pandora is enthused "I think it's a bloody brilliant idea. We need a hobby."

She nods at Digger "To be honest he wants to hibernate and waste away in Torremo- bloody- linos." She pats her cheeks "Sun's bad for my fair skin. Never saw the sun in Eindhoven when I was growing up. Too much living to do yet me. If he doesn't want to invest, I will and naturally" she considers and makes an announcement. "I will be interior décor adviser. I was always good at colour coordination and painting. I had a picture on "Neem Hart." once when I was ten."

Digger has a coughing fit and they all have a private vision of a Pandora styled club, pink and leather. The Pride.

Joby grabs the chance "We can consider that, I'm sure. It's a deal." He sticks out his hand and Pandora shakes it.

The fish that is Digger is on the bank thrashing and gasping for air. He tries one final time "Pandora if you want a hobby go to macramé with Donna. It's cheaper."

"It's Tai chi."

"I knew that."

Donna questions Joby "You know what happened with your last venture. How many cars did you ruin? "

"Yes, my little petal, we've been through all this, but thank you for raising it again. I had a brilliant flash of inspiration and it ticks all the boxes. And you my little blossom can Feng Shui the club before we open. Make sure our monkey corner or whatever is in the right place."

Donna knows he is teasing "Money corner! Absolutely essential to get the chi right."

Joby is beaming "My thoughts exactly, whatever that means. Digger are you in or out?"

Pandora enthusiastically "He's in."

Digger resignedly "It would seem I have no choice. I can't believe I am falling for it again! Pandora reconsider baby!"

Pandora turns to face Digger "Stop your whinging Digger. You're a bloody genius at these things, you've done it before and you'll do it again." She nods dismissively at Joby "God knows what would happen if we let him loose on his own. He's useless you know that. Whichever way, it'll cost us money."

Joby accepts the insult with a smile knowing his fishing expedition has landed the biggie.

He jumps from his chair, plants a kiss on Pandora's cheek and squats between her and Digger, an arm around each. "Thanks for that vote of confidence, much appreciated. What can I say? The old team together again, Little and Large, Morecombe and Wise."

Donna chuckles at him "Bungle and Zippy more like."

Joby ploughs on "We need to celebrate the reformation of the Black/Jones partnership. Digger and I will reconnoitre as soon as we get back and then, put that plan together for Ken's legal beagle."

A strange mumbling sound comes from Digger due to his head being in his hands. Joby comfortingly pats him on the back.

"In the mean time on this auspicious occasion lets splash out. Bols anyone."

The band supply the perfect soundtrack, Sonny Landreth's "Shooting for the Moon."

For the first time in ages Joby is a happy man.

*They say the sky is the limit*
*Reflected in the mirror of the mighty Mississippi*
*Shooting for the moon*
*Crash landing in the Crescent city*
*Shooting for the moon*

# Chapter 3

The rest of the weekend was enjoyable enough but pretty uneventful, apart from more beer and bols, dinner on a canal boat and more moaning from Digger about poverty and bread lines. Now, on a grey Monday morning back in Wycombe, the two friends are stood in the middle of a small back street staring at an aged, wooden double door set in the middle of three railway arches. Behind them, across the narrow street, stands an older style garage come workshop, with a motley array of cars and vans parked on the cluttered forecourt waiting to be patched up. The town planners of many years ago obviously had a grim sense of humour because Evergreen Street had very rarely seen any greenery at all. In fact, for many years locals called it Nevergreen Street. Moved to the peripherary of the town centre by modern developments, Evergreen Street was now somewhere you would walk to, rather than walk through. Once cobbled, and now potholed, it follows the disused Victorian viaduct for less than fifty yards and where many years ago several small furniture businesses thrived here, now it is flanked only by the garage on one side and the lockup on the other. Joby is smiling whilst Digger is stood with his hands on his hips, lips tight, slowly shaking his head.

After due consideration he delivers his measured verdict "I knew it would be a shit hole."

Joby is staring proudly as if at an ugly, but much loved, baby.

"This shit hole, as you so delicately put it, is our little goldmine me old mucker. Try using some of that vision you keep telling me you have. Or alternatively go and drink at The Pride. Trust me just this once."

Digger advances towards the door "Trust you? Been there, done that, thanks."

Joby is all positivity "Listen a few weeks and we'll have this place sorted."

Digger stops in his tracks and slowly turns "A... FEW... WEEKS? A few bleeding months more like, plus throw in a fumigator, a bulldozer and maybe a flame thrower. And we haven't seen inside yet."

"Don't be a miseryguts. Take a look you'll be amazed."

He unlocks the door and, with a certain trepidation, they slowly enter. In front of them lies a dirty, dusty space spanning three arches of the low viaduct. The floor is littered with debris from years gone by, the walls a mixture of brick and Victorian granite.

Joby points out his vision.

"Stage there, bar over there." He guides Digger around "Little kitchen area here. Burgers, scampi, soup in a basket." Then proudly pointing to the far corner "And over there, the bogs."

Digger is kicking over some indeterminate rubbish "Smells like someone beat you to it mate. What is that smell?"

"I do believe it's shit"

Digger has a coughing fit "I know that but what have they done to it."

Joby lets out a guffaw. They wander about some more.

"I said it was perfect didn't I."

Digger isn't convinced "Do you know what? Perfect isn't the precise word I would choose to describe this public toilet." He sighs resignedly "However, Pandora is all for it so that's that then, I have no say."

Joby decides to enlighten his friend "Did I ever tell you I've always liked her more than you?"

"More than once. Can I suggest that we get moving and put a business plan together before I suffer from the onset of sanity?"

He suddenly stops and shakes his head in disbelief "I can't believe I just said that. Ah well, in for a penny. Or in this case a hundred grand."

A beaten man, Digger's mind turns to business.

"Ok we'll do the plan tomorrow, rather I'll do the plan tomorrow. Soon as we get that passed, we need to find a decent builder. I guess we can use John. John the Builder. He's a builder."

Joby looks at his friend "And his name is John? John the Builder? You know how to do this business plan do you?"

"Done loads. And as for John the Builder well, he's a bit rough and ready but reliable. He built our conservatory, did a nice job."

Joby raises his eyebrows "Can't argue with those credentials. If he survived your missus bullying him every five minutes, then he's ok with me."

Digger's brain is whirring "Then we'll need reliable staff. And publicity. Isn't your cousin something on the radio?"

"Indeed, he is. A big noise. Record audience figures and several awards apparently."

"Then he'll come in handy. So promotional stuff is your job."

"No problems. Leave it to me."

Digger is about to comment but decides against it. He carries on with his list.

"Licences, Pandora is good at sorting out the paperwork and cutting through the red tape. Decor, that's Donna and us. For God's sake don't let my missus near it. Maybe a House band. Yes! Definitely a house band."

Joby slaps his pal on the back "As usual Digger you are spot on, brilliant. My flair and your organisational skills and it'll be Bobs your uncle and Fanny's your aunt in no time. Though these days it could be Fanny's your uncle as well."

He enthuses on "I'm really excited. My, sorry, our own bar and I can't think of anyone else I would want to do it with."

He puts his arm around his friend's shoulders "We can play any music we want. No Rap crap though, and no death metal either, Ken can rotate 360 degrees in his grave for all I care. Blues and soul that's the ticket. Stuff to make your hair curl."

He stands back and looks at Digger "Not yours of course. I bet all the big acts will be gagging for us to book them."

Digger has yet to be convinced "Mmm maybe. And we'll need a good name, something catchy."

They think.
"House of Blues has been used."
"Soul Cellar."
"Used."
"Digger's Den."
"Bollocks."

"Blues Café."

Joby is getting agitated "Not a café is it! Ok let's think laterally. We're gonna have soul and blues so how about putting the two words together, you know mixing them up blues and soul, soul and blues. "

Digger helps "What like Bloul or Slues."

Joby just stares and shakes his head in disbelief "You're amazing." Then beaming he has a stroke of genius "How about, wait for it …. The Blues Hole."

He waits for the penny to drop. Digger is screwing his eyes up thinking hard.

Joby can't wait "See what I did there, play on words. Blues soul, Blues Hole. Geddit? THE BLUES HOLE."

Kerplunk the penny hits the bottom.

Digger is unusually impressed "Nice one. Though you were always pretty sharp at The Sun crossword."

"Telegraph actually, cryptic and quick I'll have you know."

"I like it."

Joby peers at his friend through squinted eyes "If that was a compliment to little old useless me, I'll have it stuffed and mounted. We'll shove it in a case over there by the crapper."

"Ok sarky. Yes, it was a compliment. I like it a lot." He mouths it over again "The blues Hole. The Blues hole."

Then with a last look before they leave, he mumbles "And what a shitty hole it is too."

Joby pulls the door shut.

*I don't need no diamond ring*
*I don't need no Cadillac car*
*Just want to drink my Ripple wine*
*Down in the Blues Hole Bar*
*Down in the Blues Hole Bar*

\* \* \*

The subsequent trip to the solicitor's was a much more positive affair. Joby had caught the bus and was meeting Digger there. The suit is on again, as is the tie but this time without the accompanying whining. Joby is ensconced on the reception sofa reading Hello magazine circa 2000 when the door opens, and a very smart man enters wearing a Paul Smith suit and looking every part the successful executive. Joby has to look twice before realising it's actually Digger. He drops his magazine on to the coffee table.

"Good god almighty. Were you mugged by Gok Cok or whatever his name is on the way in? It is you, isn't it?"

Digger holds his hands out "What ? You think I always look like a dosser?"

Joby sees this as a rhetorical question "Well…well yeah, now you ask."

Digger shrugs off the slight "In business you need to dress appropriately Jobes, something you should learn. This is my I mean business look."

Joby looks at his own tired suit "Well I assume then that this is my I'm broke give me my money look."

Digger remains standing, smiling kindly at the receptionist who now returns the compliment. He leans conspiratorially towards Joby "I think I'm in there."

"As if! You do make me laugh sometimes. Two questions. Did you bring the plan and will it fool him?

"Two answers. One, Yes, I did and two, I don't need to fool him, it works thank you very much. It's tight but with a gale up our jacksies we can make some money."

Joby gives him a thumbs up "Good work partner. Listen today, you do all the talking and I'll just chip in when needed."

Digger has other thoughts "Actually a better idea is you totally shut up and leave it all to me. I've had you chip in before and surprise, surprise it cost me money then."

"Oh, here we go again. Listen, those magistrates were bent."

"Well, I don't believe you calling them, now what was it, oh yes, a bunch of failed middle managers and jobsworths helped the cause immensely."

"The truth hurts sometimes Digger."

"Lucky I escaped the nick after your help. I was happy with the three points. So today schtum thank's very much."

The reception phone rings and the pretty receptionist answers. She addresses Digger "Mr. Williams will see you and your colleague now."

Joby frowns at the sleight and jumps up but Digger takes the lead "Thank you so much. Come along sunshine don't lag behind."

Digger leads the way into Mr. Williams' office but Joby pushes past.

"Excuse me!"

Mr. Williams is in the same sartorial garb as before, but somehow looking possibly greyer.

"Good morning Mr. Williams nice to see you again. You're looking um ... well."

The solicitor peers over his glasses "Good morning Mr. Bl...Joby and ......Mr Jones?

Digger smiles "Good Morning."

"I barely recognised you." He points to the chairs at his desk "Please take a seat. I hope you both had an enjoyable weekend. You have a plan for me I understand."

They sit and Joby takes the lead.

"Yes indeedy, on both counts Mr. Williams. My esteemed business partner and I have thought long and hard about this conundrum and we have devised a plan that will satisfy all my sadistic uncle's requirements. God rest his pickled and twisted soul."

"Excellent."

Joby continues "We naturally took into account both the music and business aspects as requested, plus the use of the asset i.e.one lock up currently full of shite ... no, literally. This plan fulfils all the necessary criteria and as such you will be handing over the money before we leave."

Mr. Williams folds his arms and leans back "Well, I'll be the judge of that. I very much look forward to hearing what you have in mind. So, if I may borrow one of your uncle's sayings, let's rock shall we."

The boys are somewhat taken aback by the Grey Man but Joby proceeds.

"Ok. Now Mr. Jones here, in his position as financial whiz kid, will be presenting our plan today. I will be acting as his 'as required' assistant."

"Splendid. Please proceed Mr Jones."

Digger takes out a sheath of papers from his leather briefcase and places them on the desk. Joby is suddenly seeing another side to his friend.

Digger starts to speak in a serious voice "As I am sure you will be aware Mr. Williams a business plan precisely defines the business, identifies our goals and will serve as our company's resume. The basic components will include a current and pro forma balance sheet, an envisaged income statement and a cash flow analysis. It should in effect help us allocate resources properly, handle unforeseen complications and make good business decisions. Are you with me so far?"

Mr. Williams is watching him intently "Oh indeed Mr Jones, please carry on."

Digger passes a set of documents across the desk.

"Thank you. As you will see, I have divided the plan into a number of areas namely what service or product our business will provide and what needs it fills. Who are the potential customers for our product and service and why will they purchase it from us. Finally, how we will reach our potential customers and where we will get the financial resources to start our business."

Joby sits staring, mouth agape as Digger continues unabated.

"The last part is easy it's Ken's money and a corresponding amount grudgingly squeezed from myself. If you look at these documents you will see I have broken down all the various aspects into their relevant sectors. I think you will find the arguments for this plan are indeed water tight."

Mr. Williams reads on until he reaches the coup de grace.

"It's a music club, in the lock up. Interesting concept."

Joby leaps in pointing "Not just any music club it's a Blues Club, The Blues Hole, see it says it there."

As if reprimanding a child Digger stops him "Thank you Joby, if I may continue. From this plan you will see that not only have we totally fulfilled Ken's requirements but in fact have here the basis for a very successful business filling a niche market in this town."

Joby can't contain himself "Exactly. Have you been to The Pride?"

Digger turns to Joby again and is even firmer "Thank you Joby, I don't believe I nodded in your direction, did I? Any questions Mr. Williams?"

"Maybe. Let me just read this through again. Please take a seat in reception for a few minutes whilst I digest it."

The meeting is adjourned and the intrepid pair troop back out to await a verdict. Joby turns to his pal in amazement.

"When did you do all that? It was brilliant."

Digger is blasé "Mostly last night. Basically bollocks of course but you can do anything on a tablet these days. Apps for everything. Anyone with real business sense would see a few holes but I am betting on the BBB principle."

"BBB?"

"Bullshit baffles brains."

"Well, it baffled me."

"No surprise there then. Though I must say I did get a feeling there might be a good business opportunity in there somewhere. Let's get it past old misery guts first though."

They stand in silence until the receptionist breaks the mood.

"Could you go back in please."

Mr. Williams was leaning back in his seat pursing his lips as they entered and retook their seats

Joby is impatient "Well? Don't keep us in suspense. I'm sure this is what Ken had in mind for that place when he took it on. A Shangri la for the music fan."

Mr. Williams is suddenly amused.

"Really Joby, you think so? How romantic. As a long-term acquaintance of your uncle, I can tell you that he actually took on the lock up to illegally import Trabant and Lada cars from Eastern Europe. He also appears to have established a somewhat shady arrangement with the garage across the road from the lock up, which I believe is still there. But apparently like most other things your uncle was involved in, the relationship turned a bit sour on him so he cleared off. Sorry to shatter your illusion."

Joby is crestfallen "So you're saying basically he was a con man. Brilliant. And I now own a lock up across from some bloke he swindled twenty odd years ago." Then concerned "Hope they don't associate me with him."

"I think you grasp the situation." Mr. Williams leans forward "Anyway back to your plan. I've read it and I must say it's quite impressive. Mostly fiction of course." He glances knowingly at Digger.

"However, you have indeed fulfilled all your uncle's requirements as laid down in his will and if you could furnish me with your bank details, I will arrange for the transfer of the £100,000 forthwith. You do have a bank account I assume? "

Joby nods as Mr. Williams continues.

"I wish you the best of luck in your venture and I will naturally watch with great interest. I also look forward to an invitation to the opening night of The Blues Hole."

He passes a document for Joby "Please read and sign this Mr. Black."

Joby scans and signs "Brilliant, fantastic. Didn't have you down as a blues fan Mr. Williams. More a Barry Manilow man I would have said."

The solicitor smiles at Joby "Mr. Black how do you think I know your uncle? I wasn't always a solicitor. I played keyboards with Ken Black in several bands in times gone by."

He looks at Digger, knowingly "But there comes a time when you have to join the real world. By the way what did you do with the guitar? It's safe I hope."

"Safe as houses in my shed, actually? We'll stick it in a case on the wall in the club, sort of tribute to Uncle Ken."

"Nice touch. Just make sure it's safe. Anyway, gentlemen I have other clients I need to attend to so if you will excuse me. It's been entertaining."

They each gather their various papers, rise and shake hands. Joby is all smiles "Thank you Mr. Williams, see you on opening night then."

"Indeed, I wouldn't miss it for the world."

Joby strides through the reception with Digger trailing in his wake.

"Keep up Digger lots to do!"

> *All right, look at my shoes.*
> *Not quite the walkin' blues.*
> *Don't fight, too much to lose.*
> *Can't fight the running blues.*

# Chapter 4

Reality quickly kicks in. Joby hadn't realised how much there was to do, more than either of them had expected or indeed had wished for. So, over the following weeks Digger, spurred on by the thought of losing his hard-earned money, drove everyone to unheard heights of activity. Joby is enthused and had never been so busy or so happy, his feet hardly touching the floor. He was a man possessed. With Digger managing the budget with an iron fist, John the Builder was brought on board, in fact all John the Builder's family seemed to be on board. John the Builder was a local man with a shock of white hair and of indeterminate age but certainly over sixty Digger estimated. No one had ever seen John out of his old dark blue overalls that were covered with a vast variety of paint, plaster and more questionable detritus. He never seemed to get flustered and worked at a constant amble, sharing his politically incorrect views and comments to all and sundry. A man happy in his own skin.

The refurbishment plans for the Blues Hole had been drawn up, presented and approved thanks to Pandora's unique brand of persistency and the club was now a constant hive of activity. The walls had either been whitewashed or brickwork exposed and placed around, on the walls or on shelves, were various old musical instruments and pictures whilst Ken's guitar had pride of place in a perspex case above the urinals in the Gent's toilet.

This sunny morning painters, plasterers and assorted labourers were hard at work whilst Joby has collared Digger for a meeting of minds.

"Ok, things left to sort out."

John the Builder wanders past. He points his hammer across the club at Pandora and leans to whisper gruffly into Joby's ear.

"Sort out? I could sort her out, know what I mean. OI oi?"

A confused Joby turns but John silently disappears into the toilets from whence subsequently loud singing emanates. Joby stares in the direction of the racket and shakes his head resignedly "Jesus. Ok note to self, get big soundproof door on bogs."

He turns back to Digger."Ok Mr. Fixit I have the to - do list."

"Fire away."

Joby consults his piece of paper "Number one, we still have the issue of getting some decent bar staff. Now my thoughts were a couple should be enough initially, but they gotta be cheap. Profit margins and all that." He nods at Digger "See I remember the business plan."

Digger smiles "Well done. Plus, trustworthy and fit, we don't want any con merchants ripping us off and this place will be steaming some nights." Then as an afterthought "Oh by the way Ken's guitar in the bog, it's a right-handed guitar. I adjusted it."

Joby looks bemused, he doesn't care "I don't care. Right-handed, left-handed whatever who gives a monkeys. Anyway, back to important issues, staff. Knowing how lax you are in your duties I took a chance and put an advert in The Star so hopefully we should hear something iminently."

He consults his list again "And another major thing we need to address Digger is that idea of yours for a house band. Any thoughts?"

Digger affects a pondering face "Well I've been keeping my eyes open and put the feelers out but, slim pickings I'm afraid."

Joby persists "Listen we only have a couple of weeks till opening so you need to pull your finger out."

"I know that, thank's very much. I'll call around a bit more but who knows what'll turn up though."

More loud noises from the gents. Joby's face screws into a frown "Jesus has he got a camel in there with him."

Digger chuckles, pulls out his mobile and sets to finding some musicians "Dusty its Digger …. Yeah, fine thanks, Dusty do you know any good bands."

> *Ain't got no rest in my slumbers*
> *Ain't got no feelings to bruise*
> *Ain't got no telephone numbers*
> *I ain't got nothing but the blues*

\* \* \*

The mayhem continues apace. Workmen come and go nailing this, painting that. Donna is feng sui-ing, Pandora is doing whatever she wants and the club stereo is in fine working order with Sam and Dave belting it out, giving the room a good vibe.

Digger is back on the phone.

"And I tell you Dusty I have never seen one as hairy as that, totally put me off my stroke. Yeah, like a busby. Ok mate, speak later."

He finishes his call and wanders over to Joby who is sat at a small table eating a sandwich. Digger pulls up a paint spattered chair and sits astride it.

"Ok, Dusty says hello, been having trouble with squirrels apparently. So, I've called in a load of favours and managed to get a selection of bands and, in inverted commas, musicians coming down day after tomorrow. I said we'd have a look at them but don't hold your breath."

Joby munches on "Thanks Dig most reassuring. As long as it's not that guy who plays the mouth organ in the subway. You know the one? Just blows in and out. He's shite. In fact, his dog is more musical than he is."

Digger takes an optimistic tone "Hey we may be surprised. You never know."

Joby glances up at his friend "Surprised? Bloody amazed more like."

A passing John leans in and points at Donna "Amazed? I'd bloody amaze her. Did I ever tell you about…"

Joby swivels in his seat "Yes! Now clear off. What the fuck goes through that head?"

Meanwhile a slim, young man in his early twenties with long blond hair has entered the club and is standing in the doorway surveying the activity. Appreciating the music, he sways and nods his head in time with the beat.

He calls out to no one in particular "Afternoon all. Is this the Blues Hole?"

He holds up a copy of the local paper and reads out "The Home of British Blues and Soul."

Smiling, Digger looks at Joby "All yours I believe. Be gentle." He signals to the lad to come over.

As he approaches Digger stands and looks him up and down, especially the hair "What can we do for you Duffy. Job applicant?"

The boy nods. "See my colleague here" He points at Joby who is leaning back in his seat, munching on the last of his sandwich.

Over the PA Walter Troutt is filling the club with his own special brand of electric blues as the lad steps over to stand in front of Joby "Alright? I've come about the job." He points upward "This is good stuff, who is it?"

"This young man is the genius known as Walter Trout."

The boy laughs "Trout? That's a funny name, Trout."

Joby is not impressed "And who may I ask are you?"

"Mickey...Mickey Wellard."

Joby lets out a guffaw "Fuck me, Well..ard.... and you thought Trout was a funny name. At least he can play the guitar like a god."He stares at the boy "Well? Carry on."

Mickey gathers himself and reads the advert "Bar staff required for Britain's premier Blues and Soul Club. Experienced, honest and cheap a prerequisite. Must be able to handle difficult customers. No time wasters."

He folds the paper and puts it under his arm and then with a nod and a wink "That's me. It's your lucky day. You're all sorted."

Joby hasn't moved. "Riiiight. Oh good, I'm glad to hear it."

Mickey tries more bluster "Well..ard by name, Well..ard by nature they say."

Joby is most unimpressed and just sits.

The boy sees it's time to shut up "Um. I'd make a great barman, oh and bouncer."

An uneasy silence fills the space between them. Mickey looks about and continues "Nice place."

Joby "It will be. Now pardon my candour but you don't look like a barman or a bouncer to me. Perhaps an art student or a shelf filler at River Island. But bouncer, nah. So off you go and thanks for coming. I wouldn't want to keep you from your stocktaking"

Mickey demeanour changes as he steps forward forcing Joby to lean back, nearly falling over his chair.

"Listen, sir, I may have been a little bit out of order just now but I don't deserve your attitude. For your information I'm an excellent barman. I'm hard working, honest and as for a bouncer don't mess with me or you will get confirmation of my skills, the painful way."

Mickey continues in a conciliatory tone "Look, I'm offering you my services so let's stop messing about, shall we? Do I get the job or not?"

Joby takes a moment to regain his composure and then speaks in a more respectful manner. Well sort of respectful.

"Oooo listen to her. Well, Mr. Mickey Well..ard, as I can't be arsed seeing any more tossers like you and only cos you're the first, and hopefully the last, how about we say yes on a trial basis."

Mickey sticks out his hand and they shake "Ok, deal "

"I presume you have the necessary references for this prestigious role?"

Mickey nods and pulls a sheet of paper out of his trouser pocket and hands it to Joby who reads it.

"Good. We open in a couple of weeks so it's up to you to muck in and sort the bar out. We don't pay much" He nods over towards Digger "my tightfisted colleague makes sure of that, but I can guarantee it will be interesting and we'll get you some help. Come in tomorrow and sort the details out, ok?" They shake hands again.

Joby winces "Easy big boy."

Mickey says his goodbyes and Joby walks over to confide in Digger "I liked him, stood up for himself. Reminded me of me in my younger days. He'll be fine."

> *Get me a room at the Squire*
> *the local bar is hiring,*
> *And I can eat here every night,*
> *what the hell have I got to lose?*
> *Got a crazy sensation, go or stay?*
> *now I gotta choose,*
> *And I'll accept your invitation to the blues*

\* \* \*

Two busy days later Joby, Digger, Pandora, Donna and various workmen, are gathered around the tables listening to a band auditioning on the club stage. They almost finish together, almost. Joby is frustrated at what he has seen and has his forehead resting on the table. It would be fair to say that at this stage the house band auditions have not been going great. Not even been going good.

Digger is in charge of the morning's activities "Thanks guys. We'll let you know."

Joby sits up, blinks as if coming out of a stupour and comments with a resigned sigh "Not bad I suppose. How many is that we've seen?"

Digger checks down his list "Nine so far, if you count the banjo duo."

Donna has strange musical tastes "Oh I liked them. They were really good. Duelling banjos is a particular favourite of mine."

Joby looks incredulously at his wife "Darling, you liked all of them. You even liked the guy with the ukulele and the accordion with his selections from the Yiddish Song Book. Remember this is a blues bar not, Bar Mitzvah or whatever. Who's next Dig?"

Digger checks his running order "Well, according to Dusty this next lot are supposed to be half decent. Mind you they need to be cos that's it then. There aint no more."

A motley crew are wandering in setting up. They look least like a band of any they have seen so far. Joby watches in laconic amazement as they wander in.

"Well, this *is* encouraging Digger. I can safely say we cover all demographics here. Definitely have no complaints from the Equal Opportunities Commission."

He holds his hands out as they file past.

"Help the aged."
"The homeless."
"The follicaly challenged."
"Middle Earth."
"Ethnic minorities and."

He stares mouth agape at the drummer who has a mass of hair and a big bushy beard "The Muppets."

He turns to the table behind him "Is One flew over the cuckoo's nest on at The Swan?"

The band take no notice and carry on setting up. Digger chuckles "Give them a chance Joby."

Mickey who has been watching proceedings from the safety of the bar walks over with a tray of drinks, hands them out and leans into Joby singing "You can't judge a book by looking at its cover."

Joby is less than impressed "Sod off Madonna."

Donna pats Joby's arm "Be nice. They look interesting."

Joby sighs "This from someone who thought Boxcar Willy was something you caught from dirty train seats."

John the Builder is lounging feet up at a nearby table. He addresses the wives "Don't know about Boxcar Willy but you can have some Free Willy if you want girls."

Pandora who is painting her nails bright red responds without looking up "Free villy. I bet you were a bloody riot at the Edinburgh Festival John. Now please shut up before I varnish over the end of your free villy and your balletjes vallen."

John sits back with a grunt.

She continues "Do you think this lot will know any Engleburt? I love Engleburt."

Joby "Oh god I hope not! What are they called?"

Digger looks at his list "Heavenly Cow."

"Heavenly Cow? What sort of name is that? Holy Bullshit more like."

The band indicate they are ready so Digger addresses them "Ok boys in your own time."

The count from the drummer goes up "One and two and."

Digger stops them dead in their tracks" Whoa up there!!"

The opening count peters out

"A word to the wise. We've already heard six versions of Mustang Sally this morning, so something different would be greatly appreciated."

The band have a quick muffled conversation and go into a rocking blues number. It ticks on with great guitar and sax solos. It boogies along a treat. Everyone in the club is astounded as these guys are obviously accomplished and totally belie their look. The workmen dance around like uncles at a wedding, the wives even manage to get Joby and Digger up and Mickey is throwing moves with an attractive coffee coloured girl who has seemingly wandered in from outside.

Heavenly Cow finish to surprised and loud applause. Everyone including the new girl are crowding at the front of the stage. Digger's face is wreathed in a broad smile, he is obviously delighted and relieved.

"Not bad I suppose, if you like that sort of thing. Personally, I loved it. Joby what about you?"

Joby gives him the thumbs up "What can I say boys. That was great. Now we will need you available for two nights minimum a week, providing the Home let you out of course. Ok with you?"

Ben, the leader of the band (homeless category on the Joby scale) is a small, dishevelled individual. He gets the band in a huddle and returns the verdict" Guess we can do that. What's the deal?"

Joby nods towards Digger "See the banker there, he'll sort you out."

Digger climbs on the stage and addresses the band "Brilliant. Heavenly Cow, no more. You are now officially The Blues Hole Band."

Joby turns and finds himself face to face with the new arrival.

"Oh hello. Can I help you?"

She taps the local newspaper she is carrying.

"Hi I'm Safiya. I've come about the position for barperson and chef you're advertising."

"Chef?" Joby is puzzled for a second, then he twigs "Oh yes very nouveau cuisine. Well, I have to say we've been inundated with requests to work in this 4star culinary establishment, in fact had to turn down Gordon Ramsey earlier and Nadiya didn't even make it through the door."

Donna eases Joby aside and looks Safiya up and down "Don't listen to him, you're the first applicant. Do I know you darling? You look very familiar."

Safiya shakes her head "Oh I shouldn't think so, I only moved here recently. I'm staying with some friends from the Holy Saints Mission. Do you know it?"

Joby nods "Oh indeedy. Is the Reverend Ness still down there?"

"Yes, he is. I help out there and sing in his gospel choir on a Sunday."

Joby's takes this in "Gospel? Love it. Well, we need all the divine intervention we can get hold of here. Who knows perhaps you can get the Church of the Easily Led, or whatever they're called, to visit and show us the road to salvation."

He is stunned at the genius of his own thinking.

"Actually, that's not a bad idea. Bit of Gospel on a Sunday lunchtime, lovely. We could send the plate around. Church of the Easily Led, I know a few thousand who would qualify for that ministry. In fact, Nessy, well he'd definitely qualify as a member. Didn't that choir win some big competition or something a while back?"

"They did yes. So, you know Rev Ness?"

Joby smiles wryly "Oh we go back a long way. Give him my best when you see him."

Joby turns and nods towards Mickey who is singing to himself behind the bar.

"He fancies himself as a crooner as well. Who knows, play your cards right you could be the new Sonny and Cher. Any cooking experience? Ritz, Savoy, Burger King?"

"Loads" Safiya counts on her fingers "Wimpy, Macdonalds, Bigga Burgas, even a kebab van. I'd be ideal for you."

Digger has been listening and is in a hiring mood "Perfect. You're hired. We'll get you started next week."

He throws a wave towards the bar "Work with Mickey there on sorting the kitchen and bar out" He looks to see Mickey singing to himself "Oh, he's harmless by the way."

Joby throws an arm around his mate "It's all coming together. I'm starting to really believe we have a chance here me old mucker. Perhaps I've been a bit hard on old Kenny boy."

"Early days yet Jobes. Let's not get too excited eh."

Joby's brain is bursting with rocking blues.

*We want to leave you happy*
*Dont want to leave you sad*
*We want to leave you happy*
*Dont want to leave you sad*
*Want to sing some blues*
*But dont want to sing them bad*

# Chapter 5

Preparation and reparation continue apace. The days slip by and The Blues Hole slowly transforms from a desolate, dusty, vault into something resembling a blues club. Suddenly, it's time. Early morning Friday, launch day and inside the Blues Hole, as expected, there is frantic activity with builders putting the finishing touches. Joby has erected an old picture of Ken in full hair flowing, groin thrusting action on the wall behind the bar and has had John instal a strip light underneath to illuminate it. Ken's "pride and joy" guitar is in its case on the wall in the gents. Joby, Digger and Donna are generally faffing about trying to help but mostly getting in everyone's way. On stage The Blues Hole Band are practicing but with what could kindly be called very mixed results.

Digger is agitated as he calls across the club "Joby, what time are we due at the radio station?"

Stood behind the bar, Joby is having a break. Calmly swigging on a beer, he nonchalantly looks around taking it all in."Stop panicking. We don't have to be there till eleven thirty. Loads of time."

Digger is apprehensive as he leans on the counter. He points a finger at his partner.

"But we're all set, yeah? No hidden surprises like there normally are when you organise something."

"You worry too much. Have a beer."

"A beer? Bit early to be drinking, isn't it?"

"Early? Listen as a famous man once said, I can't remember who it was but he was famous, Beer is proof that God loves us and wants us to be happy. You know, when I read about the evils of drinking as a teenager, I gave up .... reading that is."

Digger turns back to face the room "Well that explains a lot then. So, it's all organised?"

Joby is unconcerned "Yeah! Of course. We've got the prime slot on Tommy's lunchtime show. Took a bit of sorting but he owes me a few favours."

Digger is excited at the prospect of being a radio star.

"Great. I wonder how many listeners we'll get. Whaddya think?"

Joby ponders "Oh I don't know, hundred and fifty, two hundred."

Digger is impressd "Amazing, two hundred thousand. Not bad for local radio. When I was playing with The ..."

Joby breaks in suddenly realising Digger's mistake "Ah no. I meant two hundred as in, you know, two hundred. Two zero zero."

He looks at Digger with a frown "You do know where he works don't you?"

Digger shrugs his shoulders as he leans over the bar "Regional radio?"

Joby explains "Wycombe Hospital Radio. We're taking blues to the sick and needy."

Digger swings around "What? When you told me were going on the radio, I was thinking something bigger like Mix or Magic or something like that."

"Really?"

"I didn't think we were gonna be talking to a bunch of sicko's. How many of them are going to be getting off their bed pans to grace our doors this evening?"

He shakes his head in disdain and points agitatedly as he turns to face the stage where the band are arguing over an ending.

"Don't need more sick buggers in here. I've got a set of jump leads out the back in case that lot keel over."

Joby finishes his beer "You need one of Donna's relaxation cd's? Listen, you ungrateful little sod, you have no idea of the effort I have been putting in. I've been working my kabuna off and this is how you show gratitude. Well thanks very much."

Digger has calmed down "Sorry."

Joby presses on with more words of wisdom "Listen, before you criticise someone, you need to walk a mile in their shoes." He pauses for effect "That way when you criticise them at least you'll be a mile away and you'll have their shoes... "

He chortles at his own joke then gets serious with Digger "There is method behind the madness here. Who works in a hospital? Think hard now." Before Digger can answer Joby carries on "Yes that's right, nurses. And who are some of the biggest tipplers around, correct again, nurses. You getting my drift?"

"Ok give it a rest I get the picture."

Mickey and Safiya have been working hard all week attempting to get the bar set up. With the band still arguing on stage Mickey wanders over to deliver an update.

"Ok boys, now I don't want to panic you but we've got no extra beers, no soft drinks, no crisps and they've sent veggie instead of beefy burgers."

Digger's calm moment evaporates and now he is now totally stressed out "So basically you're saying that unless we have a club full of tea total vegetarians tonight, we're buggered. Excellent. Well done. What a cock up."

He turns and shouts at the band who have moved on to a heated discussion about an intro.

"And it doesn't help having you bunch of tone deaf, musically challenged, amateurs caterwauling and arguing all morning. If that's the best you can do, I'll be tearing up your contract."

Joby taps him on the shoulder and quietly whispers in his ear "Digger, there is no contract."

"I'm not fucking surprised."

Joby pats his friend on the shoulder and calls over to Safiya "Safiya call the suppliers and ask for Danny. Tell him that if it isn't sorted by midday, then his missus is going to suddenly find out about him and that Polish secretary of his."

"Ok. Hey what's she like this Polish secretary, nice?"

Joby winks at Safiya "Who said it's a she."

He turns away and points at the band "And you lot quit your yapping and get it right. Otherwise." He puts his arm round Digger's shoulders "I'll turn the incredible sulk on you. Or worse his missus."

Much muttering from the stage when as if by magic, right on cue, the aforementioned Amazon that is Pandora saunters in.

Joby goes to meet her arms outstretched in a welcoming greeting "Ah Pandora my little Dutch tulip, I presume we have the licences sorted out?"

Pandora walks straight past him and kisses Digger on the head.

She turns to face Joby "Presume what you like. Seems they are almost ready but those vankers down at the Town Hall are still pre -vari-cating. I have been on the phone <u>all</u> week with no success. But they haven't accounted for me and" She thrusts her ample chest out "my enforcers."

Digger is aghast "Pandora! Behave."

"What? A girl must use all her weapons. We'll get them, don't worry."

Joby is smiling "That's my girl."

Pandora is focussed "I'm off down there now to meet that toad Thompson. He's playing the silly kont bandiet."

Joby "I have no idea what that is but it sounds painful. Do you want me to call him?"

Pandora is dismissive "Nah the little neuken gezicht fancies himself as a ladies' man so he's bound to want to go for a drink or lunch or something."

The boys ask in unison "neuken gezicht?"

"I believe in English you would say Face of the Fornication"

She heads for the door and turns.

"But I don't mind a free lunch and as men only have two emotions, Hungry or Horny, a quick Harvester and two hours of my splijten in his face should sort him out. See you later boys."

Digger is disgusted "Charming. What happened to the shy demure girl I married?"

Joby laughs at his friend's description "She was never either of those. You must be thinking of someone else."

"You're probably right."

Joby reflects "It's Mr. neuken gezicht Thompson I feel sorry for."

*I feel sorry for the guy*
*That winds up in her arms*
*He's gonna wake up wondering*
*What train just ran over his heart*
*With that little black dress*
*Those lava red lips*
*And one thing on her mind*
*She's gonna hurt somebody*

\* \* \*

Pandora pushes open the swing doors at the town hall and clacks her way across to the reception desk. Stationed behind the desk is what could be termed a "jobsworth" in a pretend uniform. All serge and gold braid. A graduate of the old school of jobsworths who attempts to ooze authority but only succeeds in oozing cheap after shave.

Pandora approaches and asks politely.

"Good morning, I have an appointment with Barry Thompson. My name is Pandora Jones."

General Jobsworth raises a finger and chooses to ignore her for about 30 seconds, preferring to read something very important on a recycling pamphlet. Slowly he deigns to look her up and then down, eventually concentrating on her chest as he points to a visitor's book.

"Now then dear, <u>Councillor</u> Thompson you say? You need to sign in madam and then I will see if he is available."

Pandora signs the book and sees that he is still staring at her chest as he tears her off a visitor's badge.

She lets out a sharp shout "Oi! Up here."

He jumps and raises his eyes

"That's it, keep them coming Colonel Knop Hoofd, six more inches, good boy, vell done. See, these are called eyes and that's where you need to be looking not at my jubblies. Now, room and floor?"

Embarrassed, he hands over her badge with a nervous cough "Second floor, room 15 madam. I'll tell Councillor Thompson you are on your way."

"Uitstekend, you do that."

She takes her badge and crosses the town hall reception area and starts climbing the stairs, her high heels echoing around the building as she climbs. On reaching the second floor she proceeds to look along the corridor for room 15.

"11,13,13a ah, here we are 15."She stops outside a door and adjusts her blouse. She knocks and from behind the mahogany door, a smarmy voice responds.

"Entrée."

Pandora pushes the door open to view a smart office. A rather short, portly man with a sponge like face and a thinning sandy hair combover rises to greet her. He is well dressed and smells of expensive cologne.

He smiles and extends his hand "Mrs. Jones, good morning. A real pleasure to meet you at last. And looking wonderful if I may say so. It seems like we have been talking on the phone forever. Not that I'm complaining of course I love an accent. Please take a seat."

Pandora lowers her statuesque body into the chair "Nice to meet you as well Mr. Thompson. I must say I didn't realise getting these licences would be such the palaver but, thank goodness, its all done and dusted now. Do you have them ready cos it's opening evening today for us, so we have a bit of a rush on."

He smiles condescendingly at her his voice dripping grease "Oh please don't panic Pandora. They should be with us shortly, barring anything unforeseen happening of course. I can call you Pandora I hope?"

Pandora smells a rat "Unforeseen? Oh, I hope not. How long do you think they will be?"

He reaches for his desk phone, wrinkles his face in a lardy smile and dials "Let's find out, shall we? Hello it's Councillor Thompson here. Do you have the Blues Hole licences ready?"

A pause. "Oh dear, really? Ok well let me know when they are please."

He leans forward, leering through podgy eyelids "A few minor technicalities to iron out, but I'm sure I can move it through." He looks at his watch "Still, perhaps we can pop out and have a bite of lunch while we wait. I am sure the council's coffers will run to a meal for such a beautiful resident."

Pandora looks at him with a raised eyebrow. She realises the game is on and he could delay the licences, so she smiles benevolently at him.

"Perfect Barry, I can call you Barry I hope? You can tell me all about yourself."

Thompson claps his hands together in delight and stands up and escorts Pandora to the door.

She stops and turns to pat him on the cheek. "As we say in Holland it all sounds een belasting van volledige stier stront."

"Splendid how quaint. It will be nice to get to know each other a bit better don't you think. Oh, allow me."

He holds the door open for her and as she passes him, he lays his hand in the middle of her back in an intimate gesture. Pandora tries hard not to gag.

\* \* \*

Digger has driven around the hospital car park four times before at last finding a spot next to the Dermatology department. Joby jumps out, locates a ticket machine and inserts all the change in his pocket to pay for two hours parking. Together they stride towards the main building. Since taking on the club Joby has adopted the Digger mode of dress. Today they are both sporting the jeans, jackets and t-shirt look favoured by would be middle age rock impresarios.

As they walk, Joby is bemoaning the cost of parking "Christ how expensive is that car park? No wonder you never see a poor Doctor."

"Is that true?"

"Well have you ever seen one driving a crappy car? No, precisely."

He stares up at the monstrosity that is Wycombe General "Don't know about you Dig but these places give me the willies."

As they head towards the main reception Digger shivers "Personally I never know what to talk about when I go to visit. Always ends up with how are you, how you feeling, how's the food, how's the hernia, ah well don't go lifting anything heavy, see you soon."

Joby nods in agreement but finds a positive "Nurses are tops though. Down to earth. Do you remember when I had waterworks problems a few years ago?"

"Oh yeah how could I forget. You had an obituary already written."

"Couldn't rely on you to do it. Anyway, they get me in to slip a camera down through my" He makes a flapping motion towards his trousers, "you know, and have a butchers inside."

Digger winces. Joby continues as they pass the ambulance bays "So, there I am on this bed with my tackle out and this nurse, nice girl mind you, has the job of squeezing anaesthetic gel down inside my" more hand flapping "you know, ready for the doctor to slide the camera in."

Digger winces some more "Don't!"

They circumnavigate some patients in dressing gowns, smoking outside the entrance "I know it made my eyes water too. Anyway, there I am flat out, goolies akimbo like some bloody Aztec offering and there she is holding my" More hand waving.

"I know"

"And she's staring down concentrating on the job in hand, so to speak. Do you know what she says? Guess. She says - Your face looks familiar." He pauses for effect "She's holding my, you know, staring at it whilst slapping gel around and asking me if we have met before! I pissed myself laughing, no I really did. Dreadful mess."

They laugh as they push through the front doors and head for the lifts. After what seems minutes, the lift doors slowly clatter open. The lift smells of antiseptic and is full of patients, some in plaster casts, some on crutches and even one old lady dragging a drip. Joby is relaxed about it all but Digger edges into a corner as if a broken ankle was contagious. The only other two non-invalids are a strikingly attractive girl accompanied by her less than attractive friend.

The lift rattles upward very slowly and apart from random coughing, silence reigns. It stops at every floor until eventually the two girls get out leaving Digger and Joby alone for the remainder of the ascent.

Joby puts forward a theory. One of many he has.

"Don't you think it's funny how good looking people always have an ugly friend. Seems it's essential in life to have an ugly friend, just to make you feel better about yourself. It's something that came to me years ago. I call it Joby's Law."

Digger knows whats coming "Don't tell me. I suppose I was your ugly friend?"

"Still are mate."

They travel the last two floors in silence until the lift doors rattle open and they step out and enter a lowlit corridor. Half way along they stop outside an office which boasts a hand written sign - *Hospital Radio – Do Not Enter*. Ignoring it, they quietly push the door open and ease themselves gingerly in. There, behind a glass partition is sat Tommy. He is on air and waves them to come around to his side of the desk. The studio is dim and windowless and is littered with the remains of earlier pizzas and coffee. They quietly sit as he makes an announcement to his audience.

"And remember, a bedpan is not a toy."

He puts on a jingle and shakes hands with the boys.

"Hi guys, how are you? We can go straight into it when this ends, if that's ok."

Joby "No problem Tommy. We're ready. Can't hang around today."

The jingle ends and Tommy is straight in.

"Today is a real treat as we have some very special guests in the studio. One of my oldest friends, Joby Black and his partner Digger Jones. Their new music venue, The Blues Hole, opens tonight. So, a big Wycombe Hospital Radio welcome guys. Tell us what your place is all about?"

Joby takes the lead. He leans forward and speaks in a sincere low voice "Hi Tommy, and a big hello to all sick people listening out there. Tommy, as I look out of your window at the rolling panorama of your very expensive car park and our great metropolis beyond…."

The other two bemusedly look around the windowless studio wondering what window he's referring to.

"I realise how privileged Digger and I are to be fit and healthy and opening up Britain's newest and hottest blues club. We're bringing blues and soul to this great town. And not before time I might add. It's been a musical wasteland too long."

Tommy affects a cheesy DJ voice "So tell me guys I guess we all know what soul music is, what with films like The Commitments but in a nutshell, how would you describe blues music? "

Digger, the musician, leaps in with enthusiasm and blurts out" Well Tommy in it's basic offering the blues is a twelve-bar form, the first four bars are in the tonic, with the seventh added in the third or fourth bar. "

Joby and Tommy have a resigned look on their faces as Digger rambles on. It all becomes just noise.

"Blah blah in the key of A, there would be three bars of A, one of A7, two of D, two of A, one of E, the next may be E or D, then A and E7. Then it starts all over again."

A minute goes by and he is still going "The words to the first four bars tend to be repeated for the second four bars, and the last four bars have different words."

He suddenly stops. There is a deadly silence as the other two stare at him.

Joby steps in "Very succinctly put Digger. Tommy the phrase the blues originally was a reference to having a fit of the blue devils, meaning 'down' spirits, depression and sadness."

Tommy tosses in a local joke "Blue devils, just like Wycombe Wanderers then."

Joby "Yeah they tend to make you miserable as well. Nowadays though, it refers to a type of music that lifts your spirits with soaring guitar solos. It makes you laugh it makes you cry, it makes your legs tremble."

Tommy with more humour "Wow. Sounds like my missuses cooking."

Joby pulls a shutup face at him and carries on regardless.

"The blues' future is assured as long as people require a rollicking soundtrack for their weekend."

Tommy tries to interrupt with another joke but Joby is on a roll.

"At The Blues Hole, we will be giving global talent a stage to show off their skills. So, people get yourselves down to The Blues Hole and experience it for yourselves."

Tommy "Great. And whereabouts is this "uplifting" club?"

Digger butts in feeling left out "Under the railway arches in Evergreen St. Opposite the garage." Hesitating, his voice gets quieter "just round the corner from Chivers and Son undertakers."

Silence reigns as Tommy takes this information on board. Joby dives in.

"Yes, it's a brilliant location. Easy parking, easy access great music, international cuisine."

It's Digger's turn to stare. He mouths "International cuisine?" Joby ignores him.

"And a great fun night guaranteed for all. Plus, for this evening only, Nurses, oh and doctors, get in free up till 9 o'clock."

Tommy "Hear that girls a free night out."

Joby continues "Don't bother to get changed, keep those uniforms on and come straight down. "

Tommy gets in quickly "Yes, well, thank you boys, we have all learned something today and it sounds fantastic. I know it will be a huge success. Why don't we have some music before we talk some more. Digger, you've brought a sample of the type of music the club will be featuring. Tell us something about it."

Digger is getting into the radio mood "This is a great example of what you will hear. It's a tune by a guy called

Sonny Landreth, an excellent talent from down south, of the USA that is, not ….. south of England. This track really ticks along and should definitely get everyone up and jumping around." He hands Tommy a compilation cd "Track 5 Tommy."

This however is the wrong track and rather than the vibrant blues of Sonny it's an old Robert Johnson track of slow blues all about being down and out, prison, death and desperation.

As it starts Joby stares at Digger "Nice one. That should free up a few more beds then."

The track eventually finishes and Tommy wraps it up "So, a big thank you to our guests today Joby and Digger and the best of luck in your new venture."

Joby "Many thanks Tommy. Hope to see you all there "

"So that's The Blues Hole opening tonight. Get yourselves down there and be uplifted. Now for all of you in orthopaedic ward 7 this is Danny and the Juniors - At the Hop"

The music starts and Tommy turns the mics off. The guys get up to leave and shake hands with him.

"Thanks Tom much appreciated. We'll see you later."

"Will do, be there about eight. Sorry about the mix up on the music but no harm done, I'm sure. Most of them would be asleep anyway."

Joby and Digger head back towards the lifts. Coming towards them are a pair of nurses. After they have passed Joby leans over and whispers to Digger. "Joby's Law mate."

> *So if you wanna be happy for the rest of your life*
> *Man, find an ugly woman and make her your wife*
> *Cause pretty girls'll have you cryin the blues*
> *But when a ugly girl leaves (she ain't nothin to lose)*

# Chapter 6

At The Harvester, Pandora and Thompson are sat in a quiet corner where they have just finished their lunch. Empty glasses abound and Thompson is a little worse for wear, with beads of sweat glistening on his forehead. Pandora, who can drink for Holland, is as sober and as glamorous as when she started.

He has moved his chair around slightly and is leaning towards her "You are a very sensual woman Pandora. But you know that. I think you and I could um ... get on very well together, if you know what I mean. I could make life very easy for you ……. or not, as the case may be of course."

She edges away.

"Oh, I get the general idea but I'm a married woman and you are a married man. I don't play around, Barry."

She puts her mobile phone on the table and presses a button. She has been ready to leave for some time.

"Thank you for lunch but I think we should be going. I need to collect those licences."

Thompson leans closer nearly falling off his seat. He leans on an elbow, face resting on his upturned hand.

"Ah. I don't think you understand Pandora. Unless you play ball with me then those licences could take forever. Now, I know a nice little hotel quite near here where we could talk over things in a more ... intimate setting." He wiggles his podgy fingers "I do a marvellous massage Pandora. I'm sure those licences will suddenly appear like… magic. Otherwise, who knows, they might never show up."

He smiles a toad-like smile "You play ball with me and I will with you. It's how it works. It happens all the time in local politics. I could tell you some stories, believe me."

Pandora stares at Thompson with disdain, imagining his head on the wall of the club "So Barry, let's get this crystal clear. You are saying that unless I, Pandora Jones, have sex with you, Mr. Barry Thompson, then you will delay the issue of the Blues Hole licences, and this is the normal way the council works? Kleine klootzak. You, a senior council official, are propositioning me a member of the rate paying public."

Thompson sits upright looking surprised at her surprise.

"Well putting it like that, yes. It's just an hour of fun. You might enjoy yourself" He chuckles "I know I will. And then we will all be happy."

"Oh, I don't think any of that's going to happen Mr. Thompson."

He leers "Ya think not? It's just fun and frolics Pandora. Greasing the wheels, so to speak."

"To you maybe but not to me. Nothing vill be getting greased today Sonny Jim."

She picks up her phone and waggles it at him "These mobile phones are great aren't they. You can do all sorts of things with them now. For instance, this little button here let's me record conversations. Marvellous.And it shows our location as well."

She holds it up and plays back their earlier conversation. She then points it at his piggy face.

Click "And this allows me to take pictures. All with a time and date stamp. Isn't technology vonderful. So, what we have here is a record of you trying to get sex in return for doing your job. You can be viral in two minutes, a Youtube sensation in five. Should make a nice story in the Bucks Free Press. They love a good sleaze story. You can kiss goodbye to that big office."

Thompson is full of bluster and indignation. Suddenly he sobers up. "You wouldn't dare. You'd be ridiculed. I am a respected member of society and you are obviously……… a tart. Just look at yourself."

Pandora smiles "Don't be fooled, Barry. Appearances can be deceptive. See I have hidden depths while you have hidden shallows. Less to you than meets the eye, so to speak. You grace a room just by leaving it. I would have this in front of every newspaper by the morning. You'd better get scrubbed up ready for some TV appearances. Which is your best side you schapen aanrander!?"

Thompson scowls and stares at Pandora.

She continues "You see, politics is supposed to be the second oldest profession, but you've shown that it bears a very close resemblance to the first. So, with no respect whatsoever, get me my fucking licences… or else."

Thompson realises this could be trouble.

"Ahem, I think we should go. I have a lot of work to do. Your licences will be waiting at reception for you. I trust that we have an understanding, Pandora."

"Of course, Barry. And again, thanks for a lovely lunch, we should do it again sometime. Are you coming this evening, I did send you an invite? You'll be very welcome and sorely missed if you don't turn up and spend a lot of money. And we wouldn't want people asking questions, would we?"

The bill is brought and settled by Thompson. They rise and Pandora takes his arm with a smile.

"I look forward to a long and happy relationship between the Blues Hole and the planning department. I am sure things will move quicker in future."

Thompson looks glum as she puts her hand on his back and steers him through the door. Mission accomplished.

> *With that little black dress*
> *Those wild red lips*
> *And one thing on her mind*
> *She's gonna hurt somebody*
> *She's gonna hurt somebody*

\* \* \*

As the boys arrive back at The Blues Hole, Mickey approaches them with a smile.

"Yo bossmen. Well, your blackmail seems to have worked, everything's arrived. We should try that more often. Tell me how did you know about Danny and the secretary?"

Joby taps his nose and winks "Helps to be old and connected Morticia. Though blackmail is a dirty word, I prefer, inducement to action."

Donna who has been hanging more crystals and comes to greet the lads "Welcome back boys. How did it go?"

Joby composes himself and begins summarising the morning's activities "Lets say, shall we, that the orders for Mogadon probably trebled after our twenty minutes. But apart from that it went fine."

Digger is indignant "That's not fair. I was very good. Might get a series out of it. Digger's Blues Hour."

"Fat chance. Oh, and Digger learnt Joby's Law about ugly friends."

Donna kisses Joby on the cheek "All my friends were beautiful in their own way."

She points at the crystals spread around "Do you like my decorations? It's all feng shuied."

Joby gazes around with a resigned look "Lovely darling, very um ….. crystally."

Digger breaks the silence "OK Let's catch up with where we are. Gather round everyone."

The list comes out again "Mickey, Safiya, all set with the bar? Beverages plus the international cuisine."

Everyone stares at Digger, Digger nods at Joby.

Joby just shrugs his shoulders. "French fries are international, aren't they?"

Mickey is ready "We're all set, bring it on."

Digger calls to John the Builder"John. Toilets finished?"

John wanders over shaking his head and sucking between his teeth and delivers his assessment.

"Well, as long as no one decides to have a major incident we'll be fine. But my advice is, get a big stick ready."

The room choruses "Urghhhhh. For God's sake. You dirty bugger."

Digger "Thank you John, most graphic and informative. I will take that as a yes boss."

Turning to the stage he continues.

"Band? If I can use that term after hearing that shite this morning. All set, raring to go? "

The band glare at him and mumble. A mixture of agreement and profanities
- Yeah
- bollocks
- dick head
- Nonce

Digger doesn't look up "Excellent.Thank you for your enthusiasm gentlemen. So, all we need to do now is to get the music licences. Nothing too serious then." He looks around "Where the hell is she?"

He tries, without success, to rouse Pandora on her mobile. Everyone stands around chatting until a few minutes later she strolls in with a piece of paper sticking out of her cleavage, and a smug smile on her face.

"All right boys? Did you miss me? Had a fabulous lunch" she looks at Joby "Have you been to a Harvester before? You should try the salad bar. Lovely." Another small parade before presenting the awaited news "You will all be delighted to know that the toad Thompson is now … vell, still a toad actually."

They all stare at her. John the Builder is about to say something as Digger intervenes.

"Not a word from anyone!!"

* * *

The day moves on apace with continued hectic activity. It's mid-afternoon and Safiya and Mickey are finishing stocking the bar and arranging the provisions in the small kitchen area.

Mickey makes small talk "So what brings you to this neck of the woods then? Not exactly Las Vegas is it."

Safiya nonchalantly wipes her hands "Oh, I'm looking for someone who I hope still lives around here."

"Anyone I'd know? Who is it, an old boyfriend?"

She polishes the bar top "Nope. It's my Dad. I've never met him, in fact, never even seen a picture of him. Though apparently there is one around."

"Wow, how exciting."

Safiya continues "All I know is that my mum was here one summer and met this guy. Nine months later… you know how it goes."

He walks round the front of the bar "And there you were? Lucky us I say."

She leans to face him "I managed to get a description out of her before she died. Seems he was handsome and a smart dresser. And obviously wasn't from the Caribbean. Hence my blue eyes."

Mickey stares longingly into her eyes "Oh yes."

"Then after her stay she went home and ….. end of story."

She delicately folds a tea towel.

"She was very independent, but now she's gone I thought the time was right to find him."

Mickey is impressed "Wow. Well good luck, be sure to let me know if I can help. You should ask Joby and Digger."

They return to unpacking buns and burgers.

Mickey continues "Anyway I'm really glad you're here. All your cooking experience will really come in handy. I'm useless in the kitchen."

She laughs a fruity laugh "Sorry Mickey I can't cook and never worked in a bar either."

"What? But you told them…"

Safiya is unfazed "I know I fibbed, but I needed a job. And you all seemed so nice. I don't know how long it will take to find my Dad so, I might as well earn some money."

She puts her hands on Mickey's shoulders and stares into his eyes.

"Oh Mickey, how hard can it be for goodness' sake. It's not exactly rocket science slapping a burger in a bun is it, chill out. So, what about you? What's your story?"

Mickey's face reddens at the closeness of Safiya and he shuffles back behind the bar."Umm. Me? Nothing as exciting as you I'm afraid. Not much to tell really. Left school at sixteen, worked in a few dead-end jobs, a few bars, that's it. Oh, love soul music, hence the attraction of being here. I got a huge collection of original 45's and LP's, you should come and see them sometime."

Safiya smiles "Yeah I'd like that."

A comfortable silence settles between them until Mickey breaks it "Then of course there's the karate."

Safiya stares at him unbelievingly looking the slim blond youth up and down "Karate? You? Never."

"Oh Yeah, been doing it since school. Needed to look after yourself in our school I can tell you. Fights every break, bullying, theft, extortion, drugs. The kids were just as bad."

They laugh as Mickey carries on "Second dan now, comes in handy sometimes in this job believe me."

Joby interrupts "OK kiddy winkies. How are the Blues Hole Bar Babes, all sorted? Listen, we don't need any dramas tonight."

He nods across at Digger who is wrestling with a cash register "Hard enough keeping him from having a heart attack. Understand?"

Safiya and Mickey look at each other. Safiya raises her eyebrows, Mickey takes the hint.

"Perfect boss, no worries. Everything is A ok. We won't let you down."

"I'm sure you won't."

He sees Donna across the club "Donna! No more ruddy candles."

While Joby races off to avert a wax overload Safiya fondly puts her arm around Mickey and kisses him on the cheek.

"Thanks so much for not saying anything Mickey."

Mickey blushes then recomposes himself "Just don't muck up, ok?"

\* \* \*

Ever since the radio station debacle Digger had slowly worked himself into a bit of a state. Normally the calm one, he is now sat by the front door where he is attempting to get the cash register to work. So far, he has hit every button, pressed anything that could be pressed and has now resorted to shaking it. If it had had windscreen wipers, he would have turned them on and off as a last resort.

"Work - you - bastard !! Why - did - I – listen – to - you – Joby. You, you……wanker! I can't even get this poxy piece of cack to function. Tonight's gonna be one huge shitfest I can feel it."

He hits the till again in frustration and succeeds in achieving nothing, apart from becoming more agitated "Shit …bastard …arse…knob."

Giving up he leans his head on the keys. Joby, who has been watching this interesting piece of performance art, calmly walks over, leans across and turns the wall plug on and stands back.

The till lights up with a loud ring causing Digger to sit bolt upright.

Joby puts a reassuring arm around his friend "There. You know what they say. If at first you don't succeed, skydiving ain't your sport. Calm down or you'll have a coronary, and I'm not doing mouth to mouth on you."

He pats Digger reassuringly on the back "Listen, it's going to be fine. It's you that's making the rest of us nervous bloody wrecks."

Digger leans back and sighs "Sorry mate it's just, you know, the money and that. I thought I was going to have an easy life."

"You are having an easy life, what's the matter with you? Trust me. It's an adventure. What's the worst that can happen? No, on second thoughts don't answer that."

Donna and Pandora meanwhile, have been hanging bits of union jack bunting over the door. Donna calls for Joby to admire her work "What do you think. Not bad eh.?"

Joby is easily impressed "Fantastic angel. Very classy."

He wonders if Joby's Law of Attraction works anywhere else. He questions Pandora "Did you ever have an ugly friend when you were younger Pandora?"

She stops and thinks. "Ja. Hanneke Van Rijn. Lovely girl, but face like the proverbial shlapped arse. Had other talents though, if you know what I mean. I can't look at a bowl of fruit now without thinking of Hanneke. Especially figs."

They all silently take this in until Joby breaks the spell. "See Digger, you are just one of many in a long noble tradition. Now, are you two girls ok about your duties tonight? Donna, you're on the till. Yours is the first face people see so use that fabulous smile. Enchant them."

He turns to Pandora "Pandora you are our hostess with certainly the mostess. Make sure they get a seat or stand them at the bar. Keep them happy."

"Vill do."

"Now Digger, who of any note do we have coming this evening?"

Digger is calming down as he checks the guest list.

"Well, there's Tommy of course. He says he's hoping to record a spot for his radio show, see if he can kill a few more off no doubt. There's Mr. Williams and then there's whatshername and her old man from the council Development Control Committee. Better keep them onside. And I invited our neighbours across the road, always handy to know."

He glances at Pandora "Your bosom buddy Thompson will be here, with his latest floosie I expect, then loads of our mates and hopefully some nurses. That's it, should be a full house."

Joby rubs his hands together "Brilliant, spot on. Well done ugly, but talented, friend of mine. Hope they're thirsty."

On stage the band start assembling their kit, tightening drums, tapping cymbals, tuning guitars and doing a sound check. The obligatory "Oner…Oner..One two." mumbled into the mics. The power lights on the amps glowing red like traffic lights and cables finally being taped down. So, there it was. The final, final preparations under way and soon the doors would be open on the inaugural night of The Blues Hole.

As Muddy Waters said:

*I'm ready, ready as anybody can be*
*I'm ready, ready as anybody can be*
*Now I'm ready for you, I hope you're ready for me*

# Chapter 7

After weeks of sweat, toil and turmoil, The Blues Hole is now open and customers are arriving. There is a growing buzz of conversation, random laughter and banter. The atmosphere is warming up. Friends, nurses (surprisingly) and so-called dignitaries, throng around the door as Joby tries to welcome them.

"Hi Tommy, thanks for coming. I'll catch you later. Mr. Thompson glad you could make it. Did you have a nice lunch?"

Thompson stops in his tracks and glares at him, his face a scrunched up piggy grimace "Are you taking the piss?"

He pushes in through the crowd dragging his blonde, leggy companion with him. Joby is perplexed at the reaction "Wonder what's eating him?" but then spies Mr. Williams arriving, resplendent in jeans, open neck shirt and a black jacket.

"Ah, Mr. Williams good to see you. Hardly recognised you in civvies, how goes it?"

They shake hands "Good evening Joby."

He looks through the door "Well this is a pleasure. I must say the club looks great." He peers some more "I don't see the guitar anywhere."

Joby points to the toilets "Safe behind closed doors Mr. Williams. I don't know why you're so worried."

Mr. Williams pats Joby's arm "Just interested. Good luck tonight Joby, Ken would be proud of you"

Joby is chuffed "Thanks very much. Catch you later."

The crowd are easing through the door as a ruddy faced older man pushed his way through. Joby recognised him as the owner of the garage across the road. He'd caught glimpses over the weeks but this was their first face to face. He approached him with a smile.

"Hello neighbour come on in, good to see you. I'm Joby Black joint owner of this fine establishment. You must be Charlie."

The man replies gruffly "You any relation to that thieving bastard Kenton Black?"

Joby maintains his smile but senses the anger "Ah. I see you knew my uncle then. Long term friendship, was it?"

"That shit scarpered leaving me with a garage full of junk cars and owing me a shed load of money. I hear he's pegged it in the states. Tough. That money is still owing, so you and I will be having a little chat. Very soon."

The smile drifts from Joby's face "Nothing to do with me Charlie. I have no idea what he was up to. I think you need to kiss that goodbye and move on."

The ruddy face is pushed within a hair's breadth of Joby's nose "Oh, do you? Well, we'll see about that. I'll be back."

Charlie turns and storms off out of the club and down the street leaving Joby staring at his retreating back.

Digger, who had been sitting people wanders up "What was all that about? Not a disgruntled customer already. We've only been open ten minutes."

Joby shrugs it off "Nah. One of Ken's old mates. Came to pay his respects. Nothing to worry about."

Digger is not convinced "Listen, anything to do with Ken is definitely something to worry about."

They leave Donna to handle the till and move further into the club, circulating and talking to the patrons. A lot of chitchat, back slapping and hand shaking is going on. Pandora is taking drinks orders and music is playing over the P.A. The atmosphere is steadily starting to grow. After much glad-handing, Joby and Digger, to great applause, eventually climb on to the stage to make a welcome speech.

Joby takes the microphone "Friends, old and new."

Great cheering and various indiscernible shouted comments from the bar area.

"Thank you for that. Welcome to THE BLUES HOLE."

More cheering. He puts his arm around Digger's shoulders "Digger and I are delighted to see so many of you here tonight. This has been a dream of ours for a long time, well a couple of months at least, and tonight, after a lot of hard graft, we see it come to fruition. We would like to dedicate tonight to my uncle, Ken Black who I know some of you will remember. As you may know Ken passed away recently."

Sounds of sympathy from the audience.

Joby waves the commiseration away "Don't be sad he had a bloody great time and died, as we all would like to, satisfied. I know he would want all of you to have a fabulous time here tonight."

Applause as Joby continues.

"Our aim is to bring you the best in Blues and Soul and to provide somewhere you can come to hear top bands and enjoy a great atmosphere. Plus, it's not pink!"

More cheering.

"I might add, we will not only be highlighting established bands but new musicians who, with your help, will be the stars of tomorrow. All of here at THE BLUES HOLE."

The crowd clap enthusiastically "I am sure Digger would like to add his welcome."

Digger is beaming as he takes over "We naturally want to thank our wives for their support, stand up girls. None of this could have been done without them."

The girls take the applause and wolf whistles.

"And to also introduce you to some really important people, our bar staff. Over there behind the bar we have the lovely Safiya"

More whistles and cheers as Safiya waves.

"And the equally adorable Mickey."

Ironic wolf whistles and cheers from the nurses as Mickey raises both arms in the air.

"They are here to look after you and I am sure you will look after them in the traditional and appropriate way."

As he is talking the band have slowly filed on stage, plugging in guitars and checking amps. Digger turns to make sure the boys are ready and gets a nod from Ben.

"Ok. Now without further ado let's get this show on the road. Ladies and Gentlemen put your hands together and welcome on stage for the very first time our own superb house band – The - Blues – Hole- Band !"

Great applause and cheering as the band strike up and rock the place with a Delbert McClinton number, a mixture of blues rock and rocking blues. Just brilliant. Joby thinks he might burst with joy. Does it get any better? Live band, Delbert, his own club. His head was spinning. Better have a beer.

*Been down in the dumps for a day or two*
*Thinkin' baby, it was time for me to make a move*
*Late night skyline that's when it hit me*
*Well, I got to have me some of that New York City*

\* \* \*

The evening starts with a bang and ticks along brilliantly. The band are on top form and everyone seems to be having a great time. The beer is flowing and the small dance floor is crowded but as is normal, with Joby and Digger involved, everything doesn't go entirely to plan. The kitchen and bar are at full stretch and, despite her best intentions, Safiya manages to cremate an offering or two whilst a flustered Mickey manages to knock a round of drinks over whilst dancing and serving at the same time. Midway through the evening, and much to her disgust, Pandora (decked out in obligatory leather trousers and knee length boots) is called on to act as temporary Dynarod representative and has the unenviable task of rushing into the toilets armed with a plunger. Screeching cries could be heard from inside followed by much flushing and continued clattering. This was also accompanied by Dutch cursing. She emerged flushed but victorious, and true to form with a flounce of her head and a shimmy of her chest, she returns to the cool blonde, dominating all around her. Queen of the kasi.

And above it all Joby floats around, oblivious to the ongoing dramas, having quite frankly, the time of his life. He had a purpose, he had success and he loved it. It was a great feeling after the numerous let downs of his earlier years. Then almost as soon the fun starts it's over, the evening draws to it's close.

A breathless Digger mounts the stage "Well everyone that's it, the first great night of many. I hope you've had a good time I know we have. If so tell your friends, if you haven't well " pointing at the audience "then shut the ... You know what I mean." Cheers and jeers.

"Once again we would like to thank everyone who has made this possible and don't forget the bar is open on selected evenings during the week. Tomorrow though it's Down to the Wire (ooohs and ahhs) and next Friday we have the fantastic Bad Influence (more oohs and ahhhs). All that's left to say is thank you, get home safely and good night."

But the crowd aren't ready to go home yet. The chant goes up "More .. more."

"OK, OK I think we have time for one last number so please put your hands together for the fantastic Blues - Hole – Band."

Wild cheering and the Band close with the classic Roadhouse Blues

*Ah keep your eyes on the road,*
*Your hands upon the wheel.*
*Keep your eyes on the road*
*Your hands upon the wheel.*
*Yeah, were going to the roadhouse,*
*Gonna have a real good-time.*

Then it's really over. As everyone files out and the hubbub dies down, Joby stands alone in the quiet. He leans against the bar his head still spinning, full of everything that had gone on. After a few minutes of thought he turns and looks up at Ken's picture and raises his glass. "I wish you could have been here tonight, you old sod. You'd have had a whale of a time, especially with those nurses." He dabs his eyes "Cheers Kenny."

*Who's gonna take your place, fill your shoes?*
*Who's gonna take your place, fill your shoes?*
*You never used to look behind you, that isn't what you'd do*
*Didn't leave a thing behind you but the miss you blues*

# Chapter 8

With the first night over and the accompanying euphoria slowly subsiding, life became a more regular round of booking bands and the daily chores of running the club. Despite the hard work, Joby had never had so much fun or been more enthused over a project. The music in his head has been rocking and upbeat, and life was good. Even Digger has stopped worrying about his investment for a while, as the club, astonishingly, was already breaking even.

The Blues Hole was becoming known around the district and on the weekends was invariably full, good crowds having a good time. Digger had expanded, and used, all his contacts and bands were eager to play. Even during the week, the bar opened a few evenings playing music over the PA to a small but faithful crowd. However, at the weekends the joint was rockin'. Buoyed by the early success the boys felt maybe the time was now right to expand the repertoire and try to attract more people on those mid week nights. They had adjourned to the Blues Hole boardroom i.e., Digger's kitchen, to examine and formulate plans.

Digger's kitchen was as modern i.e., shiny, as Joby's was traditional i.e., dated, this being a testament to Pandora and her love of glitz. Today Digger is frantically thrusting a place mat under Joby's coffee cup, attempting to avert a potential wet ring disaster.

"Sorry mate but you know what she's like about rings and stuff. Dutch Baptist upbringing."

Joby's apathy is plain to see "No worries."

Digger applies man logic "I guess being dunked in water can have a traumatic effect on an impressionable child."

Joby nearly chokes on his biscuit "Pandora impressionable? Not the word I would have particularly chosen." He points to a pile of cuttings on the side "You've been reading Ken's literary collection then."

"Yeah, some really interesting stuff in here. It would appear he was a big Hendrix fan. Not keen myself."

Joby speaks between biscuity mouthfuls, crumbs spraying "Overrated mate. All curly hair and cock. Think you either loved him or hated him. Or in my case just didn't give a stuff." Thinking on, he continues "Though, having said that, I did once have a fantastic rumpy pumpy session with an Austrian au pair to the sound of Purple Haze, but apart from that, nah not my cup of tea." He bites into another biscuit "So where is madam today?"

"At her pilot's class."

Joby looks confused "She's learning to fly? At her age? In those trousers? Fair play to the girl. Is it a Fokker?"

It's Digger's turn to look confused "Fly? No, pilots not, pilots. Stretching and stuff, elongation."

"Ah I think you mean pill-art-es."

"Do I, nah surely it's pilots"

Joby chomps on "Donna's an expert on all that stuff. Keeps on to me to go with her. Says it will sort my back out. Trouble is these classes are full of women in strange poses going hummmmmm and trumping."

Digger is about to say something as Joby holds his hands up in defence "Don't look so surprised mate. Oh yes, it's accepted, shows you're stretching your insides apparently."

"Lovely, thanks." Digger peers into the nearly empty biscuit barrel "Another?"

"Just one then." Joby takes the last one "Excellent. So, where were we? Ideas. I take it my thoughts about lap dancers are a non-starter? Go Go No Go so to speak. Lots of money in it."

Digger toys with the idea "Personally, I have no problem at all with some young lady gyrating around with her accoutrements in my face."

"Exactly."

Digger earnestly continues "And it's true it would bring in a new, and more financially liquid, range of clientele, no doubts there."

"Absolutamente."

"However, the one thing that swings it away from an overwhelming yes vote, is the undeniable fact that Donna and Pandora would, well how can I put it, castrate us."

Joby considers this option "Indeedy. Painfully true."

Digger continues "However on the plus side that could be another crowd pulling evening. Me and you having our nadgers lopped off. Small price to pay I know but something we have to take into consideration."

Joby grimaces "Good point Digs. In fact, why don't I just cross that one off the list. For the best really, quite attached to the old goolies."

They sit in silence thinking until Joby has a suggestion.

"Tell you what though, I have been seriously thinking that we should get more use out of our resident troubadours. Lazy sods."

"Troubadours? Oh, the band. Doing what? Not exactly blessed with a wealth of inter-personal skills are they."

"We need to get them out on the streets making some noise, putting the word about. Know what I mean? Singing the praises of the Blues Hole."

Digger is intrigued "Go on."

"Something to stir up some interest. Initially I thought sandwich boards. You don't see many of them around these days. Bit like white dog doo. Then I thought, the trouble with that is, our boys all look like bad police photofits so not a good image. However, they can play."

The penny drops for Digger "You want them to go busking. Correct?"

"Correct."

Digger is unconvinced "Honestly I'm not sure they're safe out alone, aren't two of them on asbo's or restraining orders or something similar."

"No worries. It'll be great publicity. And as an incentive we'll let them keep half of any money they earn."

"Very big of you"

"Look stick them in the town centre on Saturday and we'll definitely get some publicity. Those Chilean pan pipe players from Bicester do ok."

Digger shakes his head at the mention of pan pipes "God, I hate them."

Joby concurs "Me too. Donna bought a CD off them a while back and gave it to me as a birthday present. Beatles songs, on pan pipes."

"How good was it?"

Joby thinks for a second "Absolute shite. Ten pounds down the pan. Straight to the charity shop. No, me old mucker, exposure is our watchword today. Exposure."

Digger highlights a problem "I'm certain you need a licence to go busking?"

"True, but only if you want to do it legally." Joby carries on "Look don't worry about the technicalities. If you're that bothered send Pandora down to see Thompson, they seem to get on. So, you'll get them on to it yeah?"

"I'll give it a go."

"Top man. Ok, now let's have a little ponder about new ideas for getting more customers in."

Digger picks up his pencil "Yeah. Friday and Saturday nights are fine, lots of great bands booked but it's the early part of the week. We need more punters."

They sit and doodle on pieces of paper for about ten minutes writing down then scratching out. Working themselves to a sit still with enthusiasm. Digger suddenly remembers one of Joby's very few good ideas.

"I know it's a weekend thing but what about that idea you had for Sunday lunchtimes, that sounded good."

"The Church of the Easily Led? Yeah, that was a cracker wasn't it. We could give that a go, you know maybe twice a month and see what happens. Waddya think?"

"Yeah, sounds excellent."

Joby is enthused that at last one of his brain waves is being used "Do a bit of Carribean cooking maybe. Tell you what, I'll put some feelers out with Safiya and get her to check with "Brother Lurve Ness" down at the mission. If he says ok then we're on. Do they drink? I know Nessy likes a couple, well he used to?"

Digger thinks "Most of my Caribbean musician mates could certainly knock back the Red Stripe."

Joby rubs his hands together "Better get some in then. The Church of the Easily Led Sunday Gospel Lunch. A very popular ministry me thinks."

"I'm sure Safiya will help, she seems a good girl"

"Speaking about Safiya what's her deal Digger? Mickey was on about her looking for somebody or something. Your missus gets on ok with her, what does she know?"

Digger leans forward conspiratorially. "Not a lot, just that apparently Safiya's Mum lived here for a short while before Safiya was born." He shakes his head "She's probably just revisiting her roots."

Joby's not so sure "I dunno. Something about her, don't know what it is. Strange vibes. Anyway, back to the matter in hand. The weekends are sorted but like you said its mid week that's the problem. Any more ideas, any more biscuits?"

Digger gets up and puts the kettle on and rummaging in the cupboard manages to find a box of Jaffa cakes.

They doodle some more making a few notes. Their combined output eventually comes to two lines.

"So that's the sum of our total brain power is it. Tribute bands and a new talent night. Tribute bands! Jesus we're in trouble."

"People love tribute bands."

"For the wrong reasons! Do you remember that guy we saw years ago, what's his name, did that Crazy World of Arthur Brown tribute."

Digger laughs out loud at the memory "You mean Dickie Baldock! "

"That's him. We nearly died!"

Many years previously the guys went to a local village hall where their mate Dickie was due to perform. All Dickie's friends were there to support him and the small hall was extremely crowded with a buzz of expectancy in the air. Dickie and his band mounted the undersized stage with Dickie dressed as Arthur Brown (as in The Crazy World of Arthur Brown) bedecked with all the trimmings. A top hat, beard and a long coat that hid two small propane tanks on his back. He slowly approached the front of the stage where he stopped for effect. Looking around he suddenly shouts the opening words to "Fire." - I am the god of hell fire and I bring you – FIRE' At that moment two flames shot out the top of his hat and ignited the stage curtain above his head. All hell broke loose.

They both laugh at the memory. Digger is chortling "What a great night that was. Amazed the fire engines got there so quick. I didn't know I could run that fast."

Joby is back in the present, contemplating tribute acts. "I can't believe you're serious about this. What happened to our mission statement of the best in blues and soul. Oh, and the business plan."

"It's the business plan I'm thinking about. Joby, we need to boost funds. Bottom line."

"I know but we're a blues club. No tribute bands, final."

"Ok if it upsets you that much"

Grumpy Joby "It does."

Digger presses on "But a new talent night is a must."

Joby concedes "Deal. But as my old man used to say never test the water with both feet at once so, in the spirit of compromise, bash an advert in the free paper and let's see what comes up."

"Good idea. Will do."

Joby shakes his head "Though I remember the trouble we had getting a normal band, and I use the word normal in the broadest sense."

Digger chuckles "Come on. They're not <u>that</u> bad. Hey it could be a laugh and we may unearth the next big thing."

"A laugh? I could do with a few of them. Are all musicians barking Digger? Perhaps I've just been unlucky. You, Ken, the band."

Digger thinks "Mad? Umm maybe. Strange, definitely." He makes a note "So let's make Tuesday nights new talent night."

Joby grudgingly "Yeah OK"

Digger is disappointed at his friend's reaction.

"Don't sound too enthusiastic. It's quiet then and we can get acts cheap or free."

"Free's good. Whatever works." He suddenly remembers "Oh, by the way before I forget there was a note from laughing boy over the road at the garage "suggesting" I pop in and see him some time today. I was hoping he'd gone away."

"Charlie?"

"Yes Charlie. Now here's the surprise, I don't think. According to him Ken owed him money from some dodgy deal they had going."

"How much money?"

"No idea but I tell you now, if he thinks he's getting any dosh out of us then he is sadly mistaken. Never going to happen believe me."

Digger looks concerned "You be careful. He looks a rough un "

"I will. Not my fault if Ken did the dirty on him. He'll be one of many that's for sure. Still, better go and see him and get it over with."

"Want me to come with you?"

"Nah should be alright mate, thanks though. I'll see you later."

Joby stands and brushes crumbs off his lap and heads for the door as Digger sighs.

At the door he turns "And you'd better get this place tidied up before madam gets home. Absolute shambles Digger."

*Nobody knows you when you're down and out*
*In your pocket not one penny*
*And as for friends,*
*you ain't got any*

\* \* \*

Joby walked through the back streets of the town to meet Charlie, knowing that whatever was going to turn up it wasn't going to be welcome. Ambling into Evergreen Street he notices that the club lights are on, so he detours across the street and sticks his head round the door. Safiya is cleaning behind the bar.

"Hey good looking how's things?"

Her smile lights up the bar as she wipes her hands. "Not bad thanks. Just tidying up, waiting for a delivery of mixers. Where you off to?"

"Well, our friend Charlie across the road wants a chat, so I'm popping over there for a few minutes."

He steps inside and closes the door "How are they treating you at the mission?"

"They're lovely but really I think I need to find my own place."

Joby looks around and sits at the bar "Well, I'll keep my eyes open for you. In return you can do me a favour. Can you speak with the very Reverand Anthony Ness for me please? We want to set up a Sunday gospel session in the club and would like to know if he'd be interested in participating, what with him having a choir and all that. Might even rustle up a few new converts for him."

Safiya laughs "Mostly beyond saving in here but of course I will. I'll pop down after the drinks delivery."

"Good girl. Haven't seen Tony for a while, in fact not since his last wife stole all his furniture and burnt his shoes. Ah, fun times. Tell him we'll look after them with grub and stuff and a small contribution to the coffers."

He watches Safiya cleaning some glasses "So, you're planning on staying around here then? Thought you were just visiting. Not that we won't be pleased to have you for longer of course. Place needs another pretty face."

"I might be here for a while, depends. I'm on a hunt for someone who knew my mum years ago. Just to catch up. You're a local you might know him."

Joby leans on the bar "Well maybe, I know most people round here but it depends angel. When are we talking about?"

"The summer before I was born, my mum met this guy when she was here for a few months. She said he was a local lad, an absolute gent, you know the sort. Charm the birds off the trees apparently. And now I'd really like to find him."

Joby frowns "Oh right. OK. Does he owe her money or something?"

"No, he's my Dad. Mum passed away a short time ago."

Joby is taken aback "Bloody hell Safiya are you sure you want to do this? Sounds traumatic to me. Look what happened when my longlost Uncle turned up. Bloody chaos."

"No, I really want to meet him if I can."

"Well understandable I guess, but maybe better to just let things lie after all this time eh? Just get on with your life. Sleeping dogs and all that."

But Safiya is determined "As far as I'm aware he doesn't even know I exist. Mum never kept any pictures of him but apparently there's one around somewhere. I won't cause him any problems or anything like that."

"Hey listen, I'll ask about but it's a long shot to be honest. What was your mum's name?"

"Myra…Myra Thomas."

Joby goes very quiet. His eyes glaze over.

"Are you ok Joby?"

Joby snaps back to the present.

"Oh yeah, yeah fine I was just thinking but nope the name doesn't ring a bell. Anyway, I gotta dash, see you later. Lock up when you go angel. I'll just use the loo while I'm here."

"OK. I'll see you later."

Joby heads for the toilet pushes open the door and goes into the gents. The old guitar sits in pride of place on the wall. He splashes water on his face letting out a big sigh.

"Shit. Houston, we have a major problem." He drags his mobile out of his pocket and rapidly dials a number.

"Bloody voicemail. Digger? I'll tell you why Safiya is here. Two words, Myra Thomas. I'll call you back"

*Take the bait*
*You pay the price*
*It's much too late*
*For good advice*
*You know and I know that our good things' through*
*Because there's consequences for what we do*
*Consequences for me and you*

# Chapter 9

Once outside the club, Joby slowly composed himself taking in the fresh air. The name Myra Thomas was ringing in his ears along with his mental soundtrack which now was dirge like. Shaking his head, he settled himself and strode across to the garage where, on the forecourt, two big lads were working on an old banger.

"Morning, is Charlie in?"

One of the lads slowly looked up, grunted and nodded towards an old office at the back of the workshop.

Joby headed for it "Thanks, and they say the art of conversation is dead."

He knocked and pushed the door open. Charlie, resplendent in an old, oil covered overall, was sat behind a battered desk littered with oil smudged papers. He looked up as Joby walked in.

"Oh, it's you. About bleedin time too. You got the money you owe me?"

Joby ignored him and carried on "Ah Charlie. A good morning to you too. Yes, I'm fine, thanks for asking. Yep, settling in well. No thanks, no tea for me."

Placing his palms on the desk he leans forward "Now listen, I owe you sod all so don't start." Charlie is about to speak but Joby is in no mood to listen.

He ploughed on "We all want lots of things in life. Me, I want to be six foot four and guess what, that aint going to happen either. Whatever Ken owed, that's between you and him. My suggestion, for what it's worth, is to get in touch with him yourself. I believe ouija boards are all the rage these days."

Charlie grunts "Very amusing. Thirty grand. He's dead, you're alive. You owe me."

Joby sighed "Obviously the old hearing aid isn't switched on. When I said I owe you sod all, what did you actually hear? Is it the sod or is it the all that you don't comprehend? Listen, he left me sweet fanny adams, so you can rant and rave all you like but, in the interests of us all, save your breath. Just accept the fact that it's gone! He's dead you dick!"

Charlie calmly reiterated "Thirty grand. Or else."

"For fu.. Or else? Where are we, junior school? Or else your dad will beat up my dad? You'll sort me out behind the bike sheds."

"Something like that. We had a deal."

"Yes! You and him had a deal not you and me. Listen, you and my esteemed uncle had some illegal scam going so put it down to experience why don't ya. I've had a few good similar instances myself lately."

Charlie is not intimidated "I'm open to suggestions how you can settle."

Joby is exasperated "Really? Well, here's a suggestion. Get your lawyer to call my lawyer. Now that should make for an interesting chat. Love to listen in on that one. Yeah, we were illegally importing these death trap cars from Russia and then diddling the taxman. I'm sure they'll be most understanding. In the meantime, don't threaten me. I got enough worries without you chipping in."

He turns to leave. The two big lads are standing in the doorway. From behind him comes the low sound "Thirty grand, or else."

Joby is exasperated "Oh, knob off!"

He pushes past the mechanics and strides out of the garage dialling on his mobile.

"Damn, voicemail again. Digger! it's me. We need to have a chat pronto, so get yourself down to the club now, over and out."

* * *

Joby strides across to the club and tries the door. Safiya has finished and gone so he unlocks, goes straight to the bar and pours a bourbon and coke. Taking it to a table in the far corner he waits impatiently for his partner.

Fifteen long minutes later a red faced Digger rushes in.

"OK where's the fire. I was in the middle of my..."

"Don't care. Park your parts. Where shall I start? The good news or the bad news."

Digger grabs a chair "I hate these trick questions, there is no good news is there. Ok start with Safiya and Myra Thomas."

Joby sits astride a chair "Well, talk about the past coming back to haunt you. Remember Myra?"

Digger sits opposite slowly nodding "Oh yeah."

"Course you do, silly me. Mocha chocolata raver, absolutely gorgeous from somewhere round the Caribbean."

"St. Vincent."

"Really? You've got a good memory. Goodness knows what she was doing in a dump like this but anyway, she was. I still remember that night we met her at The Falcon. She was all over me."

Digger pulls a surprised face "Other way round if I remember right."

"Maybe, but who could blame her. I was a catch in those days. I remember it was a week's non stop rumpy pumpy we had. Then I go away on my hols, 14 days full board in Corfu as I recall, and when I came back, she's scarpered. Gone, never to be seen or heard of again."

He pauses "And now Safiya turns up looking for her longlost father, who it seems was an absolute charmer and had a ding dong with her late mum, Myra!"

"And you're thinking what?"

"Ipso fatso, I'm her dad. It all adds up. Unbelievable." A thought strikes him "Donna will kill me." He thinks quickly "Nope, can't tell her especially as she can't have kids. We tried long enough so let's not re-travel that rocky road."

Digger has been sat quietly watching Joby. "Let's not. Have you considered the prospect that it may not be you? I never actually put you in the charmer camp."

Joby is having none of it "Oh no it's me, I'm sure. We were at it like rabbits. She was insatiable. To be honest I was glad to get away to Messonghi Beach for a rest."

Digger tries to placate his friend "Listen don't jump to conclusions, sometimes it's best just to wait and watch."

Joby considers this option "Mmm perhaps you're right. Its gonna be hard though. I can feel it in my water. It all makes sense now."

"It only makes sense to you and your strange, warped logic."

Joby presses on "Remember Donna said there was something familiar about Safiya when we first saw her."

He gets up and paces in circles around the tables "She'll kill me. I'll have to talk to her." He pauses then circles some more "No can't talk to her. She will definitely, definitely kill me. I, am a dead man walking."

Digger isn't convinced "Course she won't. It's Donna. She's the most understanding person I know. And it was a long time ago."

Joby stops his circling "Yes you're right. It was before I met her so what right has she got to have a go at me. That's right, no right at all. I'll just tell her… later … or not … maybe."

He turns on Digger "And you can't mention it to Pandora either, promise. Promise!"

Digger lets out a snort "Yeah like that's going to happen. No bloody chance, believe me. Though be warned, she can always tell when I'm hiding something from her. Look I'll do my best. Anyway, I presume the other bad news is Charlie?"

Joby retakes his seat "Oh indeed, Charlie. Ugliest man I've ever seen with only one head. That prat thinks we're going to pay him thirty grand which he" He points animatedly at Ken's picture over the bar "apparently conned him out of! Some hope there. I told him to go whistle. Believe me Safiya is more of an issue at the moment."

Digger shrugs "Won't be me paying him thirty grand. Sod all to do with me. Is he going to be trouble cos we can do without it?"

"What's he going to do? Sue us, kill us? Don't think so. Ignore him. Donna's more likely to kill me than Charlie. And by the way looking back I partly blame you for all this Safiya malarkey."

Digger is open-mouthed "What? What are you talking about?"

"You introduced us, me and Myra. Oh yeah, trust you to get me into more trouble."

Digger is getting angry "Hang on Joby that's really unfair."

"Oh, is it?"

"If I remember correctly, me and her were getting on great until you pushed in with the big I AM and eased me out the picture."

Joby is dismissive "You were floundering."

"I wasn't floundering I was taking my time."

Joby is more dismissive "Flapping around like a big flat flounder."

"I really liked her; she was nice. We were having a decent conversation. Oh no, this is all of your own making, you and your wandering dick. Anyway, as I said you might not be her father so for goodness sake calm down."

Joby sits quietly thinking what to do.

He reflects "I can't help my past Dig. As a famous philosopher once said - I am what I am and that's all that I am "

"Is that Aristotle?"

"Popeye the Sailor."

Silence. Joby breaks it "Nah youre right, sorry Dig. God, those were good times. At it whole weekends only stopping for Final Score, Match of the Day and a takeaway from Ho's. Marvellous."

Digger tries again to settle him down "Look stay calm, I know it's against your nature, Mr Let's not do things by halves, but do try. Anyway, I've got to go. I'm meeting Ben and the boys down The Antelope to break the good news about their extracurricular activities." He sees Joby frown "Busking to you."

"Oh, ok. Good luck."

Digger stands and turns to head for the door with Joby following slowly behind. Joby pats Digger fondly on the back "Ok mate I'll lock up here. You clear off and thanks for the advice."

Digger walks slowly to his car and climbs in mumbling under his breath "Oh boy Joby if you only knew."

*To tell the truth Is a big mistake*
*Homes will crumble and hearts will break*
*Baby, why gamble when there's so much to lose*
*Because there's consequences for what we do*
*Consequences for me and you*

\* \* \*

Digger negotiates the lunchtime traffic and finds a place to park in the High Street. From here he heads behind the Corn Market to The Antelope pub. The Antelope had, in it's time, been quaint, trendy, rough and was now back to roughly, quaint again. He stands in the doorway and spies three of the band (Ben, TJ and The General) stationed at a small table in a distant corner. Pushing his way through the lunchtime crowd he addresses them.

"Hi guys. Silly question I know, but anyone want a drink?"

They reply in unison
- Cider and blackcurrant for me (Ben)
- Lager and lime ta (TJ)
- Martini and lemonade, I'm watching my figure (The General)

Digger shakes his head as he pushes back to the bar "Joby's right. All barking."

He gets the drinks and returns to the table. Pulling up a small stool, he sits and leans towards them to put his idea forward "Ok boys I need your help. Here's the deal. Anyone here object to earning a few extra bob?"

The Group responds in a positive manner.

"Jolly good, thought not. Ok, we need you to do a bit of PR for the club on Saturday mornings, on Frogmore."

Ben acts as spokesperson "What sort of PR? I ain't parading around with one of those placards like they do for the end of the world. These are the hands of an artiste. I can't go damaging them lugging one of those things around all day."

Digger is unimpressed "Yeah right. It's nothing like that. But we do need to show the locals what a fine, talented band we have at the club" They stare at him "That's you by the way. You're going to be our ambassadors. The public face of The Blues Hole."

The General understands "He means busking. You mean busking don't you."

"Basically, yes busking. Or outdoor free entertainment I like to call it. More people deserve to see your talents."

TJ is normally the quiet one "I used to make a fortune busking in Tottenham Court Road underground. Easy money. We can do that no worries."

"And you can keep half the takings."

Ben voices his thoughts "Bollocks. Have you seen the munters in Wycombe on a Saturday? If we go into the line of fire, we keep all of it or no deal. We're the ones taking our lives in our own hands."

Digger pulls a dismissive face "Just a wee bit on the over dramatic side but alright, keep all of it I really don't care. More important things to worry about. Now, we don't have a licence or anything so you're ok with this, yes?"

Ben "Yeah it'll be fine. We'll leg it if the boys in blue turn up. Though not much chance of that in this town."

The General however sees a slight problem. He leans into the group "Might get a bit of flak from the Bicester gauchos though. They see Frogmore as their patch but we'll handle them, no worries. You'll be proud of us Digger."

Digger laughs "Really? That'll be a first." Then serious "Boys listen, this is important so don't balls it up. Oh, and behave. No out on the piss the night before, right? I am not trawling around bus shelters looking for you lot, got it? Ok, another drink? General another Martini?"

"Yeah, and stick a cherry in it this time."

\* \* \*

They chat some more before Digger takes his leave and, after collecting his car, heads home. Leaving his car keys on the hall table, he nonchalantly wanders into the kitchen where Pandora is sweeping and tutting in equal amounts.

"Have you been having a party? Like the bloody varkensstal in here."

Digger is apologetic "Not a clue what that is but sorry my darling, Joby was here and you know what a messy bugger he is. I did tidy up though."

He watches her sweeping "You look nice. How was your morning precious?"

Pandora stops, casually leans her broom against a cupboard and turns to stare at Digger through squinting eyes.

"Ok what is it? What's happened?"

Digger immediately goes on to the defensive fearing the worst "What? Why would you think something has happened for god's sake?"

Pandora steps forward and stands legs astride in front of Digger. She delivers her findings.

"I can read you like a book, and a bloody boring book it is too I might add. You have your 'shit I musn't tell Pandora' face on. I've seen it too many times over the years."

Digger stays smooth "Oh, have I? Well, this time you're wrong. Nothing has happened and there isn't anything to tell. If there were, you'd be the first to know."

"Ok now I know something is up. Digger, spill the peas. You know you're going to sooner or later, so let's make it sooner and save me making your life hel op aarde"

She stares at him unblinkingly.

Digger starts to show his agitation "Will you speak English! It's like living with Derren Brown all this physco stuff! Ok, ok. It's nothing serious. It's just that Joby has a little problem at present and as his best friend, he confided in me. Ok?"

Pandora smirks "And now as your best wife you can confide in me."

Digger is firm "Pandora I can't and I won't. It's Joby's personal problem so let it rest."

He gets up to leave but Pandora blocks his way "It's another woman isn't it. I bloody knew it." She starts to pace the kitchen "That dirty little sod. And Donna such a wonderful person. He was always led by his knop. In fact, I'm amazed he's lasted this long."

Digger is amazed at her logic "What? Why would you think that? It is not another woman, so don't go making wild assumptions, ok? I am not saying any more. Just leave it."

He wanders over and opens the fridge. Pandora however will not be shaken off as she follows him, slams the fridge door shut nearly trapping his arm.

"Well, if that's your final word and you won't tell me I will have to find out through other channels. Mind, out of the way."

She pushes past him, picks up the phone and starts dialling.

Panicking Digger confronts her "You are not calling Donna, tell me you're not. Pandora don't. I forbid you!"

Ignoring him Pandora saunters into the hall, Digger can hear her talking and laughing. After a few minutes she makes a smug return.

"There, all sorted for lunch tomorrow."

She picks up the broom and slowly returns to her cleaning.

Digger is troubled "Brilliant. You know what you're like jumping to wrong conclusions. I'm telling you now if you cause problems, I will never forgive you."

"Oh, give it a rest Digger and lift your feet up. Let's get this place tidy before I start working on you properly."

\* \* \*

As the battle of minds is unfolding in the Jones' household, Joby has arrived home to hear Donna, sat in the lounge, talking on the phone. He manages to catch snippets of the conversation as he walks down the hall.

"Well getting the two fingers in was easy enough but a thumb as well was a stretch. And after half an hour of back and forth my wrist really hurt."

Much chattering on the other end "Lunch sounds lovely, I'll see you there about one."

Joby sticks his head round the door "Hi kiddo who was that?"

"Pandora. I was telling her about my ladies' tenpin bowling evening. I'm having lunch with her tomorrow; we can have a catchup. How was your morning? Are you ok?"

Joby still looks a little despondent after his shock news. He throws his coat over the bannister before ambling into the cosy lounge. He flumps down into an armchair and emits a huge sigh "Oh, morning was pretty normal. Called in the club, saw Safiya, got her to set up a meeting about the gospel lunch."

He nonchalantly carries on, wondering how to broach the subject that was filling his mind "She's a lovely girl, I really like her. Attractive too. Obviously from exceedingly good stock."

"Yes, she is nice, very sweet."

"Then by way of a total change I had a run in with Charlie at the garage who, by the way, says we owe him thirty grand. Chatted with Digger and then wandered home. As I said pretty normal."

"Thirty thousand, we owe him thirty thousand pounds?"

"Nah. A hangover from the bad old days with Ken. It'll blow over. Anyway, we ain't got thirty grand to give him so that's that."

"True. So why the long face?"

"Just a bit low today baby. Must be the weather."

He sits dejectedly with his hands in his pockets. "I was reflecting on, you know life and the Universe and thinking how maybe I should have, could have done more. Life seems to be racing past."

Donna slowly rises and kisses him on the cheek "Aww bless."

Joby continues glumly "And how I could have done more for you. Not been such a ... a waster. Then I started thinking about us and ... you know, children and such and how much you ... wanted one and what a great mother you would have been."

Donna steps back and surveys him with a worried look. "What on earth brought this on? You never seemed too bothered about kids when we found out we couldn't have any.

Listen Joby, you've been a great husband. It's never been dull, believe me. So, we didn't have kids, so what?"

Joby shrugs "I dunno. I know you would have been a wonderful mother, if your bits had worked properly of course, but what sort of Dad would I have been? Useless probably, like at everything else."

She ruffles his hair "You would have been a top dad. You're funny, kind, thoughtful, slightly mad, you tell the worst jokes in the world and any kid would have been proud to have you as their father. And now you're doing great at the club."

She holds out her arms "Come here and give me a big cuddle."

Joby slowly rises and slumps into her chest "Thanks Donna. Seriously I don't know what I'd do without you."

Donna pats his head "Nor me."

Joby raises his head with an idea "Do you think we're too old to adopt, you know, a Romanian baby or something. Or even Chinese, they got millions over there."

Donna pulls his head back down "I think having one big kid is more than enough for now."

*Trouble, trouble, trouble on my mind.*
*Trouble, trouble, way down the line.*
*I don't need, I don't need no sympathy,*
*So babe, babe, don't you, don't you pity me.*

\* \* \*

The White Hart is a country pub which plays host to ladies who lunch. Our two lovelies are sat in the grey and cream conservatory enjoying their food. The subject of Joby hadn't been raised during starters (soup and stuffed mushrooms) and they were now finishing their main courses. Pandora feels the time is right to broach the matter.

"I love liver and bacon. I know not everyone is into offal but I am. Yummy. How was your sea bass Donna?"

"Delicious, very tasty."

The waitress brings the dessert menu and they order.

Pandora enquires calmly "How's Joby? Digger says he's a bit miserable at present. Seems to think he has a few problems. That's not like him. If there's anything I can help with Donna, you know, on a woman to woman basis, just ask. You know me, as discreet as a dumb nun."

The desserts arrive and they tuck in.

Donna is picking at her lemon sorbet "Thanks Pandora, much appreciated but I think he's ok. Though he did seem a bit down yesterday after he'd seen that horrible man at the garage." She spoons a bit more sorbet "I just think he's at that male menopause age. He'll be buying a Harley soon or having blonde highlights bless him."

"Or looking at younger women. That's what they normally do the bastards."

Donna shakes her head "Not my Joby."

Pandora presses on "They'd trade you in for a younger model as soon as look at you. Bunch of vreemdgaan klootzakken. Keep an eye on him Donna. Any signs? Is he mentioning other women, changing his habits? Washing for instance?"

Donna laughs "No nothing drastic like that. He's just the same old Joby. Don't think he's changed from the day I met him."

They eat on in silence. Donna suddenly thinks.

"Though come to think of it he did talk about Safiya being pretty and nice. Attractive he said. But she is."

Pandora nods "But young and impressionable, like we were. Mark my words you keep an eye on him."

Donna chuckles "Oh he's not like that."

"Really? They all are. With Digger it's the fear factor that keeps him on the straight and narrow."

Donna isn't convinced "You know he was a lot closer to Ken than he lets on and I think it's just starting to get to him. Digger's a big help though."

Sarcastically "Oh I bet he is. The little angel. Well just be prepared is all I'm saying and if you ever need to talk then give me a buzz. Promise?"

Donna reaches across and holds Pandora's hand "I promise." Then with a smile "Fancy a Limoncello to finish off, be a bit decadent?"

Pandora feigns innocence "Me decadent? Go on then just the one."

The liquers are supped, the bill called for and paid and the two ladies part promising to do this more often.

\* \* \*

Pandora heads home at a rate of knots to confront Digger. She pulls up in the drive, jumps out and hurries indoors. He's in the kitchen as she bustles in.

"Digger where are you? Ah there you are. Why didn't you tell me Joby was shagging Safiya. It's so obvious now. The dirty old man, he should be ashamed. He's old enough to be her father."

Digger leans back on the worktop and stares at his wife. People think Pandora rules the roost but Digger hasn't lasted all these years by being a doormat, all the time. He has his rare moments.

"Funnily enough he isn't, as you so nicely put it, shagging Safiya, far from it. That's not what's wrong with him but of course you have to jump in with both feet and make the worst assumption possible."

"You would say that wouldn't you, you're his best friend."

"I am indeed and he isn't, as you keep insisting, shagging anyone."

She throws her handbag on the table.

"God knows what skeletten you two have in your wardrobes. You men are all the same with your fancy talk and your big ideas. My mother was right. He should be ashamed and so should you for protecting him."

Digger smiles "Bit OTT if I may say so. Pandora, I am telling you now, other than Donna, Joby is not sleeping with Safiya or anyone else for that matter."

"Hmmmph. Say's you."

Digger gets tough "Yes say's I. I think he has enough on his plate with Donna and her new tantric sex dvd" He puts his hand up "Don't ask. Anyway, I am telling you to stop with the stupid accusations. He is as devoted to Donna as I am to you"

Pandora loses some of her steam "Maybe but I'll be keeping an eye on you two and don't think this is the end of it. You know something and I will get it out of you little man."

Digger moves on "How was your lunch? How was Donna?

Pandora won't be diverted "Don't change the subject. It was great and she was fine. She just puts it down to Joby losing Ken and that knob across the road causing some problems or other."

Digger sees a chance to change the subject "Charlie? Yeah, he's a pain."

Pandora snorts "I saw him the other day, got bags under his eyes bigger than his testikels. Ugly sod."

Digger explains "He says Ken owed him money so he's chasing Joby for it."

"Well, he can piss right off if he thinks we're paying him out of our share. I'll shove that spanner up his klootzak right sharpish."

Digger laughs "Well we're keeping you as our secret weapon baby. Now stick the kettle on and give it a rest."

*There's something on your mind*
*By the way you look at me*
*There's something on your mind, baby*
*By the way you look at me*
*And what you're thinking brings happiness*
*Oh and it brings misery*

# Chapter 10

Saturday in Wycombe is market day. The ancient market lines both sides of the High Street. An array of stalls offers a selection, including clothes, vegetables, a man selling Daniel O'Donnell cd's and a mobile butcher's lorry where the meat purveyor mumbles morosely into a microphone, extolling the benefits of a good sausage for the weekend. With the opening of The Eden Centre people have been coming into Wycombe from as far afield as Slough, to experience the new shopping precinct. Most of them just make the one trip. If you head west down the High Street and pass the parish church you come to an open area named Frogmore. Once upon a time a large Victorian fountain graced the town end of Frogmore and the road carried buses right around square. But that's long gone, leaving a large featureless paved area lined by taxis on one side and the back of the Chiltern Centre shops on the other. It is here on this sunny Saturday that Ben, TJ and The General are setting up for a mornings' busking. A collection of instruments including guitars, a ukelele and a mandolin are tuned and ready. Bag laden shoppers are passing by and all is well with the world as no pan pipers have yet emerged.

Ben is set to go "This'll do us. No sign of Pan's People. Ok boys we'll do twenty minutes then have a fag break."

The General straps on a guitar "Stick that Gibson case down front TJ, that's it. They can chuck the money in there. Ok lads back in the time trousers. When you're ready. One and two and three and... "

They play acoustic blues, and a small crowd slowly form and start dropping coins into the guitar case. A fair sized collection of change is being amassed and a good time is being had by all until TJ spots a problem appearing on the horizon.

The Gauchos from the pampas of Bicester had arrived and seemingly, were not happy at having competition on their lucrative patch. The three of them stride menacingly towards our boys, ponchos swaying in the morning sun, straw hats pulled down low over their brows. Menacing hombres.

TJ alerts the band "I think we have some company boys and they ain't looking too happy. In fact, they are looking plain ugly."

The General slowly takes his guitar off and lays it down "I'll take the little one, follow my lead."

The crowd parts as the bands face each other in a busking stand off. Slowly they approach each other. High noon in High Wycombe.

*I'm ready, ready as anybody can be*
*I'm ready, ready as anybody can be*
*Now I'm ready for you, I hope you're ready for me*

\* \* \*

Whilst the Frogmore standoff was evolving, the unknowing Joby and Donna are in the High Street looking at colourful Indian dresses on a stall outside W.H. Smiths. Well Donna is looking and Joby is staring vacantly into the distance.

Donna holds up a beautiful scarlet cotton creation "This is pretty. Suit me you think?"

Joby rejoins the human race "What? Oh yes. Full of eastern promise angel. That colour looks really nice on you. Matches your eyes."

"Thank you darling. "She turns to the stall holder "I'll take it. Got any money Joby? If you pay the gentleman I can pop into Argos."

Joby gets his money out and grudgingly pays. He calls after Donna "I'm nipping round to see the lads on Frogmore."

He hands over the cash and saunters off down the High Street enjoying the sunshine, seemingly happy with the world. The sound of a distant police siren drifts through the air. Quickly putting two and two together and sensing a problem, he picks up the pace and as he enters Frogmore is greeted by a scene of chaos. Cd's are strewn about, a broken guitar and bits of bamboo pipe are at the feet of the band members who are slumped on a bench, where they are being questioned by a policeman. Joby smiles as he immediately recognises him as an old school chum, Billy Dawson. He looks around for Gauchos but strangely no panpipers are to be seen. Joby wanders up to the constable.

"Hi Billy? Having fun?"

Billy stops writing and turns. "Ah Joby, just the man. Was about to give you a call. Apparently, these" He nods in the direction of the trio "gentlemen, belong to you."

"Well, in a manner of speaking I suppose. I have the dubious pleasure of being their sometime employer."

He looks around at the carnage and inquires nonchalantly "Is there a problem?"

"Problem Joby? Depends what you call a minor case of assault, criminal damage and busking without a licence."

Joby picks up a cd whose cover reads - *Pan Pipes plays Beatles.*

He shows it to Billy. "If you want to talk about criminal damage look no further mate."

"I know Joby, its shit. My missus loves it though. What can you do?"

"Donna 's the same. Where are they by the way?"

"Scarpered." He closes his notepad. "Listen Joby, if it had been anyone else apart from those bloody pipe players your boys would have been in the cells by now. As luck would have it, we've been trying to get rid of them for ages. A right bleeding nuisance. All the shop owners have been complaining. There's only so many times you can hear Norwegian Wood on a whistle before wanting to shove it somewhere."

He nods towards the band "So take my advice and get them out of here, sharpish."

"That's good of you Billy. Will do."

Billy makes to leave then stops "And I don't want to see them here again unless you get a licence. Understand?"

"Absolutely, no problem."

Billy pokes a few cd's with his shoe "I better get the council cleaners down here to sort this mess out. High Heavens is the best place for all this crap."

Joby is relieved "Look, bring your missus down the club one night. We'd love to see you."

Billy heads for his car "Ok It's a date."

Joby turns and stands in front of his crestfallen musicians. He addresses them with suitable disdain "Well done team, excellent show all round. So which part of Public Relations and behave, did you not understand."

T.J opens his mouth to explain but Joby pushes on.

"No don't explain just piss off and I'll see you at the club this evening for a post mortem."

They stand and are about to go their way but Joby hasn't finished "Hold it. How much money did you make?"

TJ adds it up "Twelve pounds, thirty five."

"Go give it to Billy." He calls across Frogmore and pushes TJ to take the money over "Billy stick this in the orphan's fund or something. Now you lot, bugger off!"

They gather their instruments and start to amble away laughing amongst themselves. Joby calls after them "And don't go down the pub and start bragging about your exploits, you are on very thin ice. It's not big and it's not clever."

Joby watches them wander off and chuckles." But it is funny though." He dials a number on his mobile "Hi Digger. Guess what the boys have been up to."

*Tried busking down in Frisco, tried dancin' in LA*
*I played the blues in Chicago, boy I ran home in Santa Fe*
*I played guitar for many men, signed a deal or two*
*And all I ever got from them is the sho-biz blues*

Saturday evening at the club and it's filling up quickly. The boys had managed to book The Paul Cox Band. Paul is a brilliant blues/soul vocalist and is a favourite with many around the London area. People are filing in and the chatter level is growing. Joby is stood casually at the bar chatting with Mickey, totally unaware that across the room Pandora is glaring at him.

"Do me a favour this evening Mickey, keep an eye open for Charlie's boys from over the road. I have a nasty suspicion we might be seeing them. And look after Safiya ok?"

Mickey is totally unfazed by the request. In his mind he ruminated that maybe his opportunity to try out his karate skills was coming and, of course, any opportunity to look after Safiya would be very gratefully received "Sure no problems. Do you want me to just chuck them out or what?"

"Just act appropriately. Chances are nothing will happen but Charlie has a bit of beef with me at present and I don't trust him. So, we need to be vigilant."

Leaving Mickey, he sidles up to Safiya and affects a protective tone "Hi Safiya how are you tonight, looking fab if I may say so. Listen you take it easy this evening, if you need anything just give me a shout. Get Mickey to do the hard work."

"Ok thanks. Oh, by the way Reverend Ness says he's fine about the gospel lunch. He'll call and sort out the details with you. I gave him your mobile number. Was that ok?"

"Great."

He moves away and works his way between tables until Pandora cuts him off and furtively whispers in his ear "I'm watching you. I don't know what you're up to but believe me I have you in my sights. You…. Dirty…. Sod."

She haughtily strides away. Joby stares after her and then sees Digger coming out of the gents. He bustles over, grabs him by the arm and pulls him to one side.

"Come here blabbermouth. So, when I said you can't mention it to Pandora what did you actually think I said … was it please rush home and tell Pandora all my business?"

Digger shakes his arm free "Ow. I didn't tell her anything but like I said she has second sight when it comes to me. I just said you were having a few personal problems that's all and that it was nothing to do with anyone else."

Joby grabs his arm again "Idiot!"

Digger trys to explain his plight "Look, being Pandora, she added two and two together and got four ... and a bit. The bit being the bit she thinks you're now having on the side."

"You Dickhead!"

A flustered Digger attempts to explain some more "I told her it was rubbish but she has a vivid imagination Joby."

"Brilliant! So, she thinks I'm having an affair with someone. Anyone in particular may I ask?"

Digger shakes his head "Not really. Could basically be anyone female you're familiar and overly friendly with."

"Wonderful." He suddenly twigs "For fu.... She was watching me talking to Safiya just now. You're a knob at times you know that don't you." He agitatedly runs his hands through his hair "She probably thinks I am bonking my long lost daughter, who of course she doesnt know is my long lost daughter and all because you couldn't keep your trap shut."

"She might not be your daughter."

Joby body language shows he's getting worked up "Don't start all that again. I'm going to have to sort this out before she gets to Donna. Now go and tell her again that I am not ..you know...anyone. I've got to have a little chat with the band before they start."

Digger sees Pandora at the door. Rushing over he grabs her arm and angrily pulls her outside to lay down the law. She shakes herself free and stands defiantly glaring at her husband.

"Now listen and listen good. Joby is not having extra marital nookie with anyone so leave it alone. I'm telling you now. Pandora, drop it."

Pandora sulkily shrugs and nods back inside in Joby's direction." Look at him, shifty bugger. So, what is it if it isn't another woman? Is he gay? Is he coming out after all these years? I've seen the way he looks at you sometimes. I've always thought he was a bit light on his loafers. Is that it? Is hij een zachte toffeeverpakker?"

Digger is exasperated "Are you mad? No, of course he's not gay so just leave him alone. I wish I hadn't said anything now. You always do this. And don't go putting ideas in Donna's head either. You haven't, have you?" He stares at her "You have! For fuck's sake Pandora!"

Pandora is dismissive "All I said was for her to keep an eye on him just in case he was wandering. He's at that age."

Digger's voice is up an octave as he begins to pace "But he isn't wandering!! Well done. So, from absolutely nothing you suddenly have my best friend having an affair and his wife stalking him. Genius. If we could harness all that devious brain power of yours, we could make a fortune. You're amazing you know that?"

Pandora attacks "Well if you had shared with me like a husband should we wouldn't be in this situation. It's all your fault, as usual." She storms off back into the club.

Digger watches her and mutters to himself "Silly me. Of course, it's my fault. Wait till she hears the real story she'll have a bleeding heart attack."

At the side of the stage Joby is talking with The General about the morning's fun and games, as the rest of the band tune up.

"Ok let me get this right. When Billy turned up, you were rolling around on the pavement with a Chilean pan pipe player who, as I now understand it, is in actual medical terms, a midget."

The General strokes his beard and ponders "Or is it a dwarf? I never know what the difference is."

"It doesn't matter! So, you break free from his iron, midget grip and whack him, with a ukulele. Even as I say it, I can't believe I'm saying it. I would stake my life that the words midget, whack and ukulele have never been said together in the same sentence, ever."

The General nods "Correct again Joby. But he was trying to bite my leg the little bastard. He was like Jimmy Crankie on speed. Very tough those gauchos. They were trying to muscle in on our pitch and head-butting Ben's guitar was the final straw, so I stepped in and did the necessary."

Joby can't believe what he is hearing "He was a midget from Bicester for christ's sake. Why didn't you just hold him at arms length, or lock him in the guitar case or something. General let me give you some free advice here. In the future when armed with a ukulele think George Formby not George Foreman."

The General can't see the problem but agrees" If you say so. No harm done though Joby. Got us noticed like you wanted."

"No harm done! Why didn't you just sling them through Burton's window and get us noticed even more. And how did those cd's get all over Frogmore?"

"Oh yeah, well TJ grabbed a big box full off of them and ran off as a diversion, but the box broke. He just kept going. Didn't realise you see? Did three circuits of Frogmore before he did."

Joby looks around the club "Well as luck would have it, it looks like your jolly jape paid off cos there are a load of new people in tonight, so I guess I can't moan too much. A close call though. I'll see you all later and get you a drink."

The General climbs on stage "Cheers Jobes."

Joby turns round to see Pandora still staring at him from the back of the club. The house band are first on and it's time for the opening set so Joby takes to the microphone to introduce them.

"Good evening ladies and gentlemen. It's great to see so many new faces here this evening. A big Blues Hole welcome to you all. Anyone on Frogmore this morning?"

An ironic cheer goes up "I hear it was entertaining. Any pan pipe fans in?"

Ironic boos

"Guess not. We have a great evening planned for you tonight with two fantastic bands. Later we have the fabulous Paul Cox Band but to start us off, direct from a command appearance at Wycombe nick please put your hands together for The Blues Hole Band."

The band rock the house.

> *Well- well, sun did rose*
> *Mama, now just before the trees*
> *I said now when the sun broke*
> *Ooo-um-mm, just a'fore the trees*
> *Well, now I went to the police station, ask them*
> *Plan on gettin' me my little girl, please*

\* \* \*

The Blues Hole Band play their set and it's the interval as Joby, Digger and Donna stand by the bar chatting and chuckling about nothing in particular. It's been a good evening so far. The club door suddenly opens sharply and the two lads from Charlie's garage stride in. Both are imposing individuals, each built like the proverbial out house.

Joby walks to meet them with a welcoming smile "Evening lads what can I do for you? Drink?"

The larger of the two (Big 1) looks down on Joby and glances around the club "Shove ya drink. We just came to see what this dump was like from the inside while it's still standing."

His colleague (Big 2), proceeds to add his tuppence worth "Never know what can happen in these old places. Accidents and such, know what I mean? Death traps. Of course, you could insure against that by paying Charlie the money you owe him."

Joby although a pacifist at heart also had a streak of stubbornness and had never been one to back away. His Father had taught him at an early age that bullies need to be faced. "Yeah right, like that's ever going to happen. Listen boys I don't want any trouble so why don't you just leave. Go off an enjoy your Saturday night and let us enjoy ours, eh?"

Mickey, who has been observing what's happening, has slowly edged round from behind the bar. Big 1 steps forward towards Joby just as Safiya is passing by with a tray of drinks. He barges her roughly out of the way but before Joby can react, a banshee cry, a flashing arm and fist lays Big 1 out.

Joby and Mickey stare down at the prone figure, groaning on the floor at their feet, and then at a heavily breathing Donna, who has executed a beautifully speeded up tai chi movement and flattened him.

To avoid any more trouble Mickey grabs Big 2 before he can move. They all stand over Big 1 who is still on the floor holding his face. There is a moment of stunned silence as Donna rubs her hands together.

"See I said it would come in useful someday."

Joby stares her open mouthed "Bloody hell Donna, that was brilliant!"

Big 1 tries to rise from the floor "Du bloke my dose."

Donna can't understand his mumbling "What did he say?"

Mickey helps translate "I believe he said du bloke his dose."

She claps her hands together "Excellent. Joby, I bloke his dose."

They stand and watch Big1 stagger to his feet and totter towards the door.

Joby is impressed wih his wife's heroics "I believe you did angel. Right on the old conk. Tell you what I'm coming with you next week." He gently pushes the groaning man through the door and out into Evergreen Street.

"Ok laddo off you go and tell that imbecile you work for that if anyone, and I mean anyone, threatens or touches my family again then they will personally answer to me, or even worse." Pointing at a beaming Donna "Her. Got it?"

Escorted by Mickey Big 2 is pushed to follow his mate. He turns and points at Joby. "You'll regret this."

"I very much doubt it. Mickey, please make sure they don't come back "

Mickey watches them slowly walk away and then returns inside where he questions a beaming Donna.

"Wow what do you call that move."

Donna goes through the movement at normal snail like Tai Chi speed.

"Mmm. I think it was Turning Body Strike the Hammer Out, or was it Parry, Punch, Withdraw and Push. One of the two. I always get those two mixed up"

Mickey laughs "Well either one, it certainly worked that's for sure."

Digger gives her a hug "And do we all feel better now?"

Joby does "Much. Some people are only alive because it's illegal to kill them."

The club settles back down to some normality as Paul Cox takes to the stage. Pandora, who can actually kill a man, given enough time, has been watching the whole episode and has been taking mental notes.

She pulls Digger to one side "Interesting don't you think. Joby's calling Safiya family now! Dirty little hondelul."

"Pandora, I don't know what that means but I'm pretty certain it's not nice!"

# Chapter 11

Despite her physical exertions the previous evening Donna is up early pottering around in the kitchen getting breakfast. Joby eventually manages to rouse himself and after consuming his bacon and eggs is attempting to complete his assigned task tasks of changing the bed linen. As any man will know this is an almost impossible task of Herculean proportion and within minutes Joby has most of his body immersed inside the duvet cover. Being forced to leave her duties due to the inordinate amount of crashing, banging, cursing and swearing upstairs Donna sticks her head round the bedroom door and sees that assistance is required.

A muffled cry "Is that you Donna? Help me out here slugger."

She extracts him from the offending bed cover and takes pity "Out of the way, it's easy. "

Within one minute as if by magic the bed is crisply tidy "There like I said simple."

Joby is chastened "To a super hero maybe but to a mere mortal it's like wrestling with an octopus."

Donna beams "I was a hero wasn't I." She flexes her fingers "Hand hurts a bit though." She points to a small bruise "Have to get some rescue remedy on it."

Joby holds her hand rubbing it gently "I would have leapt in but you were like lightening. Wham bam thank you ma'am. Very proud of you, and somewhat amazed and maybe just a little bit scared. You're not going to be jumping out and lumping me one every time I don't do the washing up are you?"

Donna laughs and playfully punches him on the chest "Don't be silly. I just use my powers for good. No one attacks my man."

"Listen I'll be paying Charlie a reciprocal visit. Unless of course you want to go."

"Nah, it's not worth it. I wouldn't bother."

"No way. He is getting a serious bollocking believe me. That is not happening again. Oh, what time is it angel?"

"Coming up to eleven."

Joby gets his jacket from the wardrobe "Hey I gotta shoot. I'm meeting Digger down at the mission to chat about the gospel lunch. Be nice to catch up with Tony again."

He heads down the stairs. Donna calls after him from the landing "Give him my love. Who's he married to now?"

Joby sits on the bottom step putting his shoes on "God knows. Last I heard it was some young thing from Slovenia, or was it Slough. Anyway, somewhere East of here. Number three or four I think, I lose track."

"Well don't you start getting any ideas about trading me in young man."

Joby stops tying his laces, pauses and wrinkles his brow "What makes you say that?"

"Just joking."

He stands to leave "Well don't joke about that sort of thing. It's not funny."

He exits quickly out the door and into the Sunday morning sunlight, heading into the town centre before the going gets any more difficult.

*I'm trouble in mind,*
*baby you know that I'm blue,*
*but I won't be blue always*
*Yes, the sun gonna shine,*
*in my back door someday*

The Cherish Gospel Chapel is hidden away behind the Swan Theatre, between the British Legion and Bucks University. It's in an area that, in years gone by, was the most picturesque part of the then Chepping Wycombe but somewhere that is now dominated by a flyover and a subway. Joby rounds the corner to see Digger pacing up and down in front of the Chapel doors. Even from across the road he can hear the vibrant sound of the choir. The building itself was an authentic single story 1970's dirty red brick block, who's design hadn't troubled any architect. It appeared to have just been dropped into a space where the planners had no idea what else to put. It was one of those buildings that always manages to look grubby around the windows, no matter how many times they are cleaned and its muddy red bricks seemed to dull any sunshine that manages to circumnavigate the overpass. Despite all this it is much loved by its congregation and especially by the Rev Tony Ness. Joby and Digger had known the Rev for many years, way before he was called to the cloth. A tall, slim, good looking man, he had found God late in life which he felt offset his discovery of the joys of women much earlier. Before his conversion he had managed to navigate his way via a considerable number of Wycombe's finest females. Married four times, with several children he had now finally settled down and grown into a leading light in the Carribean community, respected by many and quite rightly deeply proud of his ministry.

Joby crosses the road to be cheerily greeted by Digger.

"Morning. How are you?"

Joby stops in his tracks at the edge of the pavement a bemused look on his face "What? How am I? Well thanks to your big gob and that mad dyke hopper you're married to, how I am is up shit creek without the proverbial. I'm certain Donna thinks something nasty is going on."

Digger shrugs his shoulders "Something is going on. Just not what you think she thinks is going on. My advice, talk to her and explain it all. You could be worrying over nothing you know. Though after last night, watch that right hook of hers "

Joby shoves his hands in his pockets "You're no help. I am not worrying over nothing but, for once, I agree with you. I'll do it this evening. I'll quietly explain that it was before we met and it was just a holiday fling and it changes nothing."

"Well except that now she has a stepdaughter of course."

Joby is aghast at this idea "Bloody hell stop complicating things, I never thought of that. Jesus." He thinks briefly and finds the good side "Though she always said she wanted a daughter, so it might not be as bad as we think." He ponders "See I said there was nothing to worry about."

Digger stares at him shaking his head.

Joby pushes the Chapel door open "Come on don't just stand there gawping let's go in and catch the end of the service. Sound great don't they."

They gingerly tiptoed into the main hall and stood, quietly at the back, as the music filled the air and washed over them like a dark warm bath. The Chapel was full. A sea of brightly coloured outfits spread out before them. As the song came to an end Rev Ness leant on the lectern to preach, well, berate his flock.

"So, you need to ask the Lord to save you, you need to admit your sin - not just be sorry for it. You need to turn away from it and be willing to leave it for good."

The congregation respond with a loud "Praise the lord."

Digger whispers to Joby "That's you he's talking about."

"Sod off."

Tony continues "If you have done that, the word of God says that we are to confess, with our mouth - why not tell someone today? If you want to talk to me about your soul and you want to be saved, I'll be here for as long as you want."

Digger is convinced "Did he know we were coming cos it sounds very much like you?"

Joby glowers.

Tony isn't finished as he admonishes them "If you're a backslider and you want to come back to the Lord, do something! Speak to me, but whatever you do: repent."

Digger totally convinced whispers again "Oh yeah, now that definitely is you."

Joby leans into him and hisses in his ear "Will you shut up!"

A Halleluiah echoes around as Tony wraps it up "Go in peace Brothers and Sisters and remember Jesus came into the world to save sinners. Amen."

The congregation begin to file out shaking hands with the Reverend as they leave. Amongst them is Safiya who when she spots the boys gives them a coy wave and smile. Joby and Digger smile and wave back then move to one side, a little self conscious at being the only white faces in the room. As the last person leaves, the Reverend Ness approaches them nodding his head and holding his arms out.

"Ah, two sinners who are way beyond redemption." He hugs them both.

Joby slaps him on the back "Yeah? I'm not the one on my fourth wife. A very rousing sermon you old devil, I almost felt the need to be sanctified, almost. How are you?"

Tony is all teeth and smile "Joby I'm great." He turns to Digger "And Digger how are you? How's that woman of yours? Did I hear right that you'd retired with a big payday."

"Retired? I wish. The woman is much the same Tone which, as you know means rampaging around causing trouble."

Joby concurs "Tell me about it."

Tony laughs "Well, if you ever get tired of her and want me to redeem her soul give me a shout. I can show her a new way."

"Yeah right. I'll keep that in mind."

Tony turns his attention to Joby "And the wonderful Donna? I hope you're looking after her."

"Oh yeah. Keeping her in the lap of luxury as always. She sends her lurrrve by the way. You know of course Digger and I have the new blues club."

They slowly walk to the front of the chapel. Tony stops "Indeed. I've been meaning to get down there but been a bit busy here. Going ok?"

Joby stands behind the lectern" Going good but we need to expand our footprint. Did Safiya mention our idea for a gospel lunch? Could be good for business for you, if you know what I mean. Raise awareness, new souls to save."

Tony smiles "Ah the lovely Safiya. Yes, she mentioned it. Sounds promising Joby." He takes a more serious tone "Now you've known me a long time and you'll know that, despite all my previous, lets call them, waverings, I am passionate about my church so anything that helps is welcome."

Tony directs them towards a door in the corner "Let's go and sit in the vestry."

The vestry turns out to be a small room at the back of the chapel with just enough space for the three of them to squeeze around an old desk. Joby starts talking logistics.

"So, if you finish here around noon could you and the choir be with us by one?"

"No bother. Now there are twelve in the choir so will the stage take us, there's some ample ladies in our group."

Joby doesn't see a problem "Perfect, all round. No pun intended. We've got a piano as well if you need it"

Digger "Have you got a pianist or will you need the band?"

Tony leans back with a look of concern "To be honest Leslie our pianist, you remember Leslie, well two sessions a day would finish him off. Your band, are they any good?"

Digger laughs "Joby has his own views on that but they're not bad."

"They have their moments believe me. Have you been on Frogmore lately?"

"Ah. Don't tell me any more. How about they join choir practice on Tuesday for a run through."

Joby "No problem. Actually, we have a free night Tuesday so why not do it at the club. The band will be there, they owe me a big favour after yesterday. Listen we're calling this venture "The Church of the Easily Led Gospel Lunch." Any objections?"

"None at all. Sounds good to me. And we all know people who could join that church."

Digger "Everyone says that."

Tony continues "And we can sell our CD's?"

Joby is enthused "Absolutely, as long as no panpipes are involved. I'm gonna get some Blues Hole T-shirts printed so I'll get some Church of the Easily Led ones done at the same time." He thinks "Oh and we'll put some posters up in the town. Listen you tell your people about it Tone and we should have a good turn out."

Tony puts his bargaining head on "So what do we get out of this, apart from the joy of salvation for the easily led and selling a few cd's."

Joby pretends to ponders and puts forward his first bid "Well I thought 5% of the takings and a free lunch."

Tony snorts "Joby please don't insult me. 30% and free lunch and drinks."

"And you a man of god! 10% a free lunch and drinks for you."

"Make it 25% and we have a deal."

Digger chips in "Are you sure you work for the man upstairs?"

Joby knows where it's going to end "20% and we revisit it after 4 weeks, ok?"

Tony nods and they all shake hands.

Digger is thinking of his stomach "Now what about nosh? What are we going to give them to eat?"

Before Joby can speak Tony breaks in

"Don't say fried chicken!"

Joby argues "Your Mum's was the best! What then, cos there'll be a load of hungry people there."

Digger "Well I love a nice black sausage, no offence Tone, so how about a BBQ. I've got, well Pandora's actually got, a swish one at home we can use. She won't let me near it. I presume Safiya will be singing so Mickey can look after it. He'll look nice in a pinny." So, they agree on a BBQ.

Tony looks at Digger then at Joby "You know Safiya thinks her father comes from Wycombe."

Joby glances at Digger who casually replies" Yes, we'd heard something along those lines."

Tony looks questioningly, firstly at Digger and then at Joby "Did either of you know her mother by any chance?"

Joby bluffs "Nah, not me, and you're a fine one to talk with your rod of god. Not sure I did know her. You Digger?"

"Umm. Don't think so."

To their relief Tony thankfully drops the subject "Ah well I am sure it will sort itself out. Anyway, back to business. So, we'll do about an hour after everyone's got their food."

They are all happy especially Joby "Excellent. Tony it's a pleasure doing business with you. I really am excited about this. Anything else?"

"No don't think so. I have to head off to see some of my flock now but let's catch up after Tuesday's get together."

The three ease out of the vestry and amble towards the main door. Digger walks ahead talking over his shoulder "I'm off to meet Pandora down the Eden centre. Apparently, she has nothing to wear, apart from the three wardrobes full, but those are winter clothes it seems."

Tony accompanies them to the door "Well have fun and peace be with you"

The boys leave Tony to lock up and stand on the kerb. Joby throws out a worry he has "I wonder if we'll be damned for lying in a chapel."

They part company as Joby heads for home, Gospel music in his head whilst Digger heads grudgingly for his expensive lunch date with Pandora at the fabulous Eden Centre.

*Hold fast the hope that's in you*
*Don't always trust your eyes*
*Sometimes it takes a long time to see it as*
*A Blessing in Disguise*

\* \* \*

An hour or so later, Digger is ladened down like a Santorini donkey and is grumbling for England. Pandora, in customary boots, jeans and tight jumper, is striding along heading past Next, as he traipses grudgingly in her wake. Suddenly Digger decides enough is enough. He stops and calls after her "My arms are aching. Can we go home yet?"

No response "Can we sit down at least? Can we have a cup of coffee?"

Pandora eventually stops, turns and strides back to confront him. He takes a small step backwards as she reaches him "Want, want want! I have never heard anyone moan as much as you over a little shopping."

Digger stands forlornly bags around his feet "A little? That woman in House of Fraser thought Christmas had come. I'm not made of money you know."

"Yes, you are. Listen we didn't work all those years so as to sell the business and not enjoy it. What are we down to? The last five million? You are a gierig beetje stront when it comes to money." She turns on him and strides off again.

Digger collects his bags and trots, trying to keep up "I have no idea what you just said but I know it's insulting. Listen I'm just thrifty. Slow down."

They reach Starbucks. Pandora nods to the tables outside. "Sit there while I get us some coffees, you stingy weinig duivel!"

Digger gratefully plonks himself down on a spare seat and watches passers by, whilst inside, Pandora joins the queue for drinks. After a few minutes she returns to find him staring idly into space.

"A pfennig for them. You seem very preoccupied today Digger."

Digger blinks back to the present as she deposits the coffees on the table "Just thinking about Joby and before you ask no, I am not telling you."

Pandora waves her arms in annoyance "Oh Digger you're driving me mad. So, he's not bonking and he's not gay. Is he ill? Is he dying, is that it? Has he got an incurable disease? Is it catching? You're not denying it, is that it he's going to die."

She stares intently at Digger's passive face looking for something that isn't there "Oh Digger, poor Donna. A widow." She starts to sniffle.

Digger's patience is about spent "Oh for god's sake Pandora. He's not dying. I might kill him one day, but no he is not dying, not yet."

She sniffles some more. Digger relents "Baby stop blubbering, it makes that beautiful face all puffy." He sees an escape route from his current misery. "Look drink your mocha choca frappaloca, or whatever it is you have, then we'll head home and you can have a nice soak in the jacuzzi." He hands her some napkins which she blows loudly into.

"Thank you, Digger. That's a nice idea. I'll put my panpipe music on. I know how much you like it."

Digger mutters to himself "Jolly good, that'll be lovely then."

*I went and I did some little thing wrong,*
*That's why I had to go and write this song*
*'bout throwin' out the baby.*
*You're throwin' out the baby,*
*You're throwin' out the baby with the bath-water blues.*

\* \* \*

Joby meanwhile has arrived home and is ensconced in his front room, eating toasted crumpets and drinking tea. An old Sunday tradition in the Black household.

"Yummy, I love a hot crumpet and that's why I love you"

Donna reminisces "Reminds me of when I was a little girl. Sunday afternoon with the radio on, sat with my Mum and Dad. All trying to guess what was number one in the charts."

They sit in the comfortable silence eating, until Joby plucks up the courage to broach the delicate subject of Safiya.

He sits forward "Donna I need to talk to you. There's something I really have to tell you."

Donna puts her plate down and sits forward on the edge of her chair "Ok."

Joby struggles to find the right words "Um well...er it's like this um...It's a long story..."

Donna helps him "Joby just tell me. Is it another woman?"

Joby is horrified at the thought "What? God no... well not in the way you mean. Why would you think that?"

Donna plays coy "No reason. Ok carry on."

Joby starts at the beginning "When I was a teenager, surprisingly, I was a bit of a lad with the ladies and one summer, I met this girl and, you know, we, well you know!"

"You had rampant rumpy pumpy?"

Joby frowns and is slightly afronted "Well I wasn't going to quite put it like that, but yes. Now I must say it was a long time before I met you, and I haven't strayed since we met."

Donna nods and pats his knee" I believe you."

"Anyway this." He searches for the right word "fling, didn't last long because I went off on holiday, Messonghi beach Corfu, full board, very nice and when I came back, she'd gone."

"Ok and this fling has what bearing on what you are going to tell me?"

"Well to be honest, we were at it like rabbits for a week or so before I went off and well, it seems she then got pregnant and now her, my, daughter has turned up and is looking for her father, namely me. I didn't know I'd put her in the club Donna, honest."

Donna looks very seriously at him "Did you take precautions?"

"Oh yeah very careful but you know those things aren't one hundred percent."

Donna is thoughtful "Mm and who is this daughter?"

He hesitates "Well…..It's Safiya. Though she doesn't know I'm her father, yet."

"I see, and that's why you've been especially nice to her lately."

Joby is surprised "You noticed?"

"Women do. You know Pandora thinks you are having an affair."

"She's Dutch and mad, in either order, take your pick."

They sit in silence, Joby biting his lip, Donna thinking.

Joby is worried "Are you ok angel?"

"I'm fine. Joby but in the light of that news, there is something I need now to tell you."

Joby frowns wondering what is coming next "Ok, fire away."

"I don't know how to say this but well you can't be her father."

Joby is insulted at this slur on his manhood. "Can't be her father? Why not? Like I said those johnnies aren't foolproof. And we were pretty….. active."

Donna smiles "I'm sure you were."

She sits even further forward "Joby, you know when we were trying for a baby and we had all those tests?"

He raises his eyebrows "How could I forget? Never filled so many plastic tubs in my life. Muscles like Popeye."

Donna shakes her head "Quite, and when it turned out we couldn't have any, I said it was because I could'nt conceive. I said it was me."

"Sure. Hey, I never minded. It was you I felt sorry for angel. I know how much you wanted children."

"Well, Joby, I wasn't being exactly honest."

A long pause.

Joby's brain is now churning "What does that mean, not exactly honest."

"Joby it wasn't me who couldn't have kids. It was you. It's you that's sterile."

"What, that's not possible!"

Joby can't take this in so Donna tries to help as he sits with a look of extreme puzzlement on his face.

She turns "See that stone Buddha over there." She points to the corner by the door" He has a higher sperm count than you. They said it was almost a world record for lack of sperm. You were shooting more blanks than a starter at the Olympics. Apparently, you would have always been like that."

Joby is indignant "That can't be right. I was prolific, if you know what I mean."

"Joby it's quality not quantity."

He still can't absorb this information "You said it was you. I believed you. All these years. Why?"

Donna leans forward and puts her hand on his knee "I did it to protect you Joby. I thought it would just be too much for you to take. You'd just been made redundant for the first time and things weren't going great. You were down and I knew what pressure you were under, so I took the decision so you'd think it was me."

He finally gets it "So you did it for me."

"Yes of course. Why wouldn't I? "

He thinks for a second "I bought you a new eternity ring on the back of feeling sorry for you. You cheeky sod! That's fraud."

"I know and very nice it was too. I did it cos I loved you Joby and to be honest, at that time I was stronger than you. You've taken your fair share of knocks for me over the years and what did it matter if it was you or me. Neither of us was going anywhere."

Joby sniffs and furrows his brow," Oh Donna. I don't know whether to be angry or sad. I thought I had a daughter, and you had a stepdaughter. A ready-made family."

Donna smiles at the thought "It would have been nice but hey, we have each other and that's always been enough for me."

A small smile spread over Joby's face "Yeah. Me too."

Then Donna adds with a smile "And as I said, having one big kid is enough anyway."

They sit in comfortable silence. Joby dabs his cheek, taking in the revelations. Suddenly he sits bolt upright as a thought races around his brain.

"Well, if it isn't me who the hell is it?"

He lays back in the chair, thinking, names running through his head.

*From a teenage lover, to an unwed mother*
*Kept undercover, like some bad dream*
*While unwed fathers, they can't be bothered*
*They run like water, through a mountain stream*

# Chapter 12

And so, the week starts again. It's Monday morning and at The Blues Hole Mickey is silently cleaning glasses and arranging the various bottles when Safiya saunters in, glorious in cerise. Pleased to see her, he gladly leaves his chores to give her a hug.

"Hey Safiya how ya doing? Have a nice Sunday?" His day suddenly brighter.

"Very nice Mickey thank you, how about you?"

"Oh yeah good. Had a karate competition, came third so not bad. What did you get up to?"

She hangs up her coat and puts on an apron ready for work "Well I went to chapel yesterday; in fact I saw Joby and Digger there."

Mickey is taken aback at the thought of his two bosses even knowing where a chapel was "In church? Those two? Are you sure you weren't hallucinating?"

She laughs her tinkling laugh "They went to speak to the Reverend about arranging the gospel lunch. I think it's all on for next Sunday."

"Really? Well, I hope they're going to pay overtime."

They are interrupted as a happy tuneless whistling precedes Joby, who almost skips in with a big self satisfied smile on his face. It's amazing what a reprieve can do.

He greets them both warmly "Good morning my children and how are we all today. Personally, I'm on top of the world ma!"

Mickey confronts him "Yeah we're fine Joby thanks. Safiya says the gospel lunch is on."

Joby pats him on the arm "Certainly is our longhaired lover."

Mickey sees an opportunity for a monetary opportunity "Double time Sundays you know."

Joby just smiles "Absolutely."

Mickey curses "Bloody hell if I knew it was going to be that easy, I'd have asked for triple time."

"Yeah, let's not push it shall we. What are you like cooking on a BBQ Nigella?"

Mickey thinks for a second "No idea, never cooked on one. Why?"

Joby slaps him on the back "Well there's always a first time and Sunday's gonna be yours."

Mickey is not impressed "But I can't cook. Get Safiya to do it."

Joby was prepared for this objection "Ah, Safiya is singing with the choir but Donna or someone will help if you get stuck. Can't be that hard though if Digger does it."

He turns to Safiya with a big smile "Looking great today. Loving the pink. Waddya think Mickey doesn't she look fab?"

Mickey immediately goes the same colour as Safiyaes beautifully fitting top.

"Um…errr yeah"

"Thanks. I'll help if I can Mickey." She moves on "Oh Joby my Aunty has found that picture of my mum with my dad I told you about. She's sending it to me."

Joby rubs his hands together "Brilliant, I know I can't wait."

Safiya "It's really exciting. I wonder if I look like him."

"He'll be good looking if you do. Bring it in as soon as you get it. Perhaps we can help identify him for you"

The group disperses as they all go about their morning business and after a while Digger and John the Builder enter the club.

Joby greets his chum "Morning Digby. Hey John to what do we owe this pleasure?"

"Bog door's loose so I'm reinforcing it."

He heads towards the toilets where, with much hammering, he proceeds to start work on strengthening the door. Joby and Digger take a seat by the stage where it's quieter.

Joby is all sweetness and light today. He nods towards the toilets "Good old John. Nice of him to call in."

Digger is curious why Joby is still walking and not in the hospital. "How did it go last night with Donna? You still look in one piece Any hidden bruising?"

Joby shakes his head "Nope, none. One of the strangest evenings I've had for many a year. Firstly, I tell Donna about Safiya then she tells me I can't be her Dad as I'm like a seedless Jaffa."

"What?"

"Apparently all along it's me that can't have kids, not Donna. Medical impossibility. Less pips than Tesco's grapes it seems. So, it appears Safiya isn't my daughter. Great news, eh? Eh?"

Digger tries to disguise his disappointment "Well I guess so. Weren't you upset? Her keeping that from you."

"A little but she only did it to protect me and, well, we're used to being just the two of us so, no point worrying."

Digger is very flat "Suppose so. I'd have been livid. So, it's not you?"

Joby stares at his friend surprised at his lack of encouragement "Well thanks for your support. Don't sound so disappointed. I thought you'd be pleased for me."

Digger "No, I am, I'm really pleased for you…. not for me though."

"Ok you've lost me now. Why not for you?"

Digger shifts in his seat, an uncomfortable look on his face. Time to come clean.

"Well, you wont like this much but you know when you cleared off to Corfu, well."

"Yeaaaah"

"Myra and I sort of got together. Just the once, the night you left."

Joby's frown deepens "And when you say sort of got together you mean what exactly? Had a drink got together. Had a meal got together?"

"Not exactly. Don't make me spell it out. You know, together."

Joby's voice goes up an octave "You had sex with my girlfriend?!"

"Well hardly your girlfriend. You'd cleared off with whats-her-name, Susan Taylor, to Corfu. So, I thought you'd broken up with Myra and it would be ok"

Joby is appalled "Be..Ok? Beside the point, I think. Oh, I can see it now. I bet you were like a rat up a drainpipe."

Digger goes on the attack "Hey, don't forget I met her first. You stole her from me and it was only one night. I think it was probably mostly sympathy on her part. So, you see Safiya could be my daughter."

Joby thinks for a second and adopts a concerned look as he interrogates his best friend "Did you take precautions?"

"Oh yeah, you know me. I wore two."

Joby laughs out loud "Two? Bloody hell Digger even your tadpoles couldn't force their way through two layers of latex."

"So, you don't think it's me then?"

He tries to reassure Digger "I very much doubt it. Safiya is good looking for a start. Methinks Myra might have been a bit of a gal. Anyway, Safiya says her Aunty is sending a picture of her Mum and whoever the father is. So, we'll soon find out. But through two? I think not."

Digger contemplates "Now I think back it was over a bit quick. Not even sure I, you know, got it in properly. So, you're not angry at me? "

Joby is too relieved about his own situation to care much "Nah. Course not but don't get any ideas in the future."

He thinks for a second "I wonder who else could be in the frame?"

Digger throws out some names "Could be Paullie, he loved the ladies, or Fricker, dirty little devil or how about Elvis Keith, he put it about."

"Elvis Keith? Bloody hell, Myra may have been a raver but she wasn't blind! Still, no use worrying mate we'll find out soon enough. I would almost 100% guarantee it isn't you."

The banging has ceased and John the builder wanders over to update the boys on his handiwork

He pulls up a seat and joins them "There, that should keep the noise out, or in as the case may be. You could crap a pot bellied pig in there and no one would know."

Joby shakes his head at the total unawareness of the builder "Always a nice choice of phrase. Thanks John."

John doesn't do irony "Pleasure. Enjoy."

John collects his tools and heads off to his next lucky customer. Joby watches him leave then turning back to Digger broaches the subject of Charlie, their belligerent neighbour.

"I'm going to see Charlie for a little tet-a-tet in a minute. Wanna come?"

Digger is all for it" Oh yes indeedy. I can tell you now, we are not being bullied by him. He needs to know who he's messing with."

Joby smiles at his friend's bravado "Come on then, let's get it over with."

*Lord it's a down right rotten*
*low down dirty shame*
*The way that you treated me*
*Lord I know I'm not to blame*

They head out of the club and cross the narrow road to the garage, where Charlie is stood watching one of the mechanics tinkering with an engine. The younger man has a plaster across his nose and some nasty bruising. Joby hails his belligerent neighbour.

"Oi numpty."

Charlie looks up

"Good to see you know your name at least."

Charlie wipes his hands "Waddya you two want? You brought my money?"

Digger walks over and slaps the mechanic on the back "How's the dose today. She sure packs a punch don't she. You must be sooo embarrassed. Floored by a little lady."

The lad wipes his hands, sneers at Digger and slinks inside.

Charlie watches him slope away then turns to address the boys "So, have you brought my money?"

Joby is confounded "You never cease to amaze me, Charlie. You are probably one of the stupidest people I have ever met and believe me I have met a few in my time. No, we haven't brought your money and we won't be bringing your money."

Charlie steps right up to Joby. Face to face "Now listen you."

Joby puts an admonishing hand up "Ssshhh be quiet for once. You listen and you listen good. I'm generally a very peaceful person but any more incidents like Saturday night's episode and you and I are going to fall out in a very, very big way. Do I make myself clear?"

Charlie takes a step back with a puzzled look "What incident. What are you talking about? I don't know nothing about any incidents."

"Charlie, I thought you were stupid before but now I know you're a complete idiot. As I said any more trouble and I'm coming looking for you."

Digger peers around Joby" Yeah and me too."

"Thanks Dig." Joby takes a step towards the garage owner "So, let this be a final warning. You are getting no money, as there is no money plus, you touch my club, my friends or my family again and I will find you and I will hurt you. Do you understand?"

Charlie is nothing if not stubborn "Don't threaten me you nonce."

"Threaten? Oh, it's not a threat it's an absolute cast iron assurance. And pass it on to those monkeys who work for you. There won't be another warning."

Charlie blusters "You have no idea who you're dealing with do you?"

Joby turns and as he walks away sends his final warning "No more, you understand?"

Charlie shouts at their retreating backs "I want my money and I want it quick"

Joby mutters he strides off "Fucking Idiot."

*So I will tell you now*
*And I won't say it again,*
*Don't mess with me*
*Oh baby, don't mess with me*

\* \* \*

They head back into the club for a stiff pick me up or two.

Digger places two shot glasses on the bar and fills them with bourbon. "Can you believe that guy. Incredible. Even made out he knew nothing. Good job he didn't try anything, I was ready."

Joby takes a sip "I don't trust him one bit. There's just something about him, apart from being a crook. I know people." Another mouthful "What on earth did Ken want to get involved with him for?"

Digger refills the glasses "Who knows. Anyway, we warned him off so that should be the end of it."

Joby's not convinced "I doubt it. He's waited twenty odd years so I think we'll be hearing more from Charlie boy."

Digger gets back to business "More pressing issues. We have lots to do to get ready for the weekend so let's forget about him for the time being, I've sketched up a couple of designs for t-shirts. They're in my man-bag."

Joby is at a loss "Man - bag? What the hell is a man-bag?"

"It's fashion, nothing for you to worry about."

Digger gets his bag from the side of the stage and pulls out some pages. On them are a variety of drawings of logos and script for the Blues Hole and the Church of the Easily Led. He lays them on the bar for Joby to look at.

Joby looks them over "Not bad. I didn't know you were an artist."

"Don't you remember? I did art at evening classes. It was very interesting and educational."

Joby remembers alright "Oh yes of course, the art classes. If I recall Jenkinson told you they were using live nude, female models so you switched from German and the next thing we all know is, that you've bought a white smock and about fifty quid's worth of brushes."

Digger shrugs and shakes his head "Waste of money. All we ended up painting was a bowl of fruit and some old age pensioner. Most disappointing. I was never good at wrinkles or bananas."

"Well, you must have learned something cos these aren't bad at all. Especially those two." He holds up a page.

On it is written –

> *Blues and Soul*
> *at*
> *THE*
> *BLUES HOLE*

and

> *I'm A believer*
> *at*
> *The Church*
> *of the*
> *Easily Led*

Digger takes it off him "Yeah those are the two I like. Simple but effective. I thought black t-shirts with blue lettering for The Blues Hole and white t- shirts with blue for the Church."

"Yeah, that'll work."

"Ok I'll get a hundred done of each. "

"Excellent. What about the posters?"

"I'll knock some up and put them around the town."

Joby is impressed "I don't care what anyone else says, I like you. You do have a talent."

Digger smiles "Thanks, I live for your approval."

\* \* \*

That evening at Chez Jones, Digger and Pandora are relaxing in their lounge talking about the day.

"How was the chiropractor angel?"

"He cracked me around. Very strong hands. I didn't know I could get my legs in that position."

"Then where did you go?"

"Oh, popped into town, went in M & S then The Eden and then I took some of your old clothes to Oxfam. I must say they didn't seem too impressed Digger. Very reluctant."

Digger is appalled "Not my denim jackets, I hope. They're worth a fortune in those vintage shops! "

Pandora is dismissive "Oh I can't remember. There may have been one or two in there. The lady said they were really only fit for dusters. How was your day?"

"Yeah, it was ok. Joby and I went and saw Charlie and warned him off."

Pandora scrunches her face up "He is a very nasty man. He has the face als een buldog die piss van een distel likt."

"In English please."

"Um…Like the bulldog who is licking the wee wee from the thistle."

Digger shakes his head "Obviously. Very descriptive. Oh, and you'll be pleased to know Joby's problem has sorted itself out so you won't have to worry anymore."

Pandora is suddenly attentive "So they found a miracle cure for his illness then, that's nice. Or was it his gayness or is it he has been dumped by the other woman."

"Funnily enough it's none of those, but he's ok now. Lucky chap."

She pouts "Why you saying lucky chap. You are a very lucky chap Digger, you have me, this lovely house, your health, our wealth. Don't you think you are lucky?"

She jumps up and heads to the kitchen.

Digger calls after her "Yes my little Dutch tulip I am very lucky, I know that." Then under his breath "Let's hope it holds out."

*Well, I ain't been loved but four womens in my life.*
*Well, I ain't ever loved but four womens in my life.*
*Well, my mother and my sister, sweetheart and my wife.*

# Chapter 13

Digger very gratefully puts aside paternity issues and presses on regardless throughout the week. He buries himself in sorting out t-shirts and distributing posters that proclaim the forthcoming assembly of souls and anything else that will take his mind off of his impending doom. As arranged, the band have their evening with the choir for what turns out to be, wonders will never cease, an excellent rehearsal. Everybody is happy and everything seems to be coming together ready for the gospel lunch. It is now Friday morning and Digger and Joby are struggling to move a large BBQ into the club for safe keeping. After much huffing, puffing, grunting and groaning they gratefully deposit it in a corner at the back of the bar.

Digger is not used to such manual work "Bloody hell I'm knackered. Stick it here for now then we can shift it outside Sunday morning."

They manoeuvre it into the vacant space and stand and look around the club. Joby still has to pinch himself most days to realise what he is doing. From having no future to being a club owner in a matter of months, well who'd have thought it. He wanders around, a smug look on his face.

Passing by the toilet he stops to inspect John's repair work.

He opens and shuts the new door a few times nodding approvingly "He did a good job on that, nice and solid."

He notices Ken's old guitar hanging inside on the Gents wall, a sad reminder of his departed uncle. He nods at it and calls out to Digger "Do you know what, that's starting to grow on me a bit."

Digger joins him to look "Well it was your Uncle's Joby."

"Suppose so. And at least it fills a gap and it's in no one's way up there. A talking point whilst having a pee I suppose. Did those T-shirts arrive?"

"Yeah. I picked them up this morning. Come and have a butchers. You'll like em."

They leave the toilets and go back into the bar where Digger opens a large cardboard box, digs deep and holds up a t-shirt. It's white with bright blue lettering on the front

Joby is impressed "That's brilliant Dig, really good. They'll go like hot cakes. This could take off in a big way. And the Blues Hole ones?"

Digger delves deeper inside and pulls out the house merchandise and holds it up against himself.

"Waddya think?"

"Good stuff. Really good, well done old chap." He glances at his watch "Damn I promised to call Tony just to catch up."

Mickey ambles over to look and he and Digger slip on t-shirts as Joby fishes out his mobile and wanders outside.

"Hi Tony - Yeah good thanks. Just checking to make sure all still ok for Sunday. - Brilliant. Good rehearsal with the band I understand – Yeah, all barking – Nope, all ok here. The t- shirts look great by the way - OK. See you Sunday."

He finishes his call but suddenly his attention is caught by activity across the road amongst the old bangers, where he sees Charlie, clad in his customary dirty blue dungarees, emptying the contents from the boot of his car. Joby quietly watches with interest as Charlie takes out two petrol cans and places them just inside the workshop door and then goes back for what appears to be a box of assorted empty bottles which he carries in and places next to the petrol cans. Joby is intrigued as he watches his adversary go about his business. No rocking blues in his head now just strange ramblings.

*I've got an achin' in my heart*
*Arson on my mind*
*I'm gonna burn your playhouse down*
*I've got a badly broken heart*
*I've had it from the start*
*You're giving me the run around*
*Now if you play with fire*
*It's a-sure to burn*

\* \* \*

Sunday morning dawns bright and warm. Digger and Mickey have carried, or rather dragged, the BBQ outside and are now struggling to make sense of it.

Mickey stands back and addresses Digger "I would have thought that as this was your BBQ you might know how to work it."

Digger straightens up "Really? Nah this is Pandora's. I never get involved with her toys. She's the driver. I have though received special permission to use it today" He points inside the BBQ "I assume the charcoal goes there."

Mickey holds his hands out "Who knows? Where is she then?"

"Tarting herself up. She'll be down later. Let's not bother her eh, cos she'll just run us ragged. Best we just do it ourselves. Much simpler."

Mickey holds his hands out "Sure no worries. Show me that instruction book again. You get yourself round the back."

Digger stations himself as Mickey begins to read aloud.

"Ok, Step 1 - Make sure that you are using an easy clip-on regulator."

Digger stares intently and fingers a few things "Possibly. If we knew what a regulator looked like?"

"Beats me. Ok. Step 2 - Make sure that the regulator, whatever that is, is switched to the 'off' or disconnect position, all taps on the appliance are closed and the connecting pipe to the appliance is correctly fitted."

Digger has a bemused look on his face and having found some tubing is flapping it around.

"Again, possibly. Looks ok to me."

Mickey continues "Put the regulator on top of the cylinder valve."

Now Digger really is bemused. He kneels and peers inside "Cylinder. Ok what cylinder?"

Mickey is exasperated "The gas cylinder. The gas cylinder that works this thing!"

Digger pokes his head over the top "There's supposed to be a gas cylinder? Well, who'd have thought it. I thought we just chucked some charcoal in, poured petrol or whatever on and whomph. I bought loads of charcoal. Gas and charcoal, well I never. OK problem solved. We need gas."

He gets his phone out and dials "Pandy apparently there's supposed to be a gas cylinder with this BBQ where is it? - well, that's not a very nice thing to say to your husband. Who taught you that word?! - He should just stick to fixing bog doors – yes, I'll get my useless arse down to the DIY place immediately Love you too baby, kissy."

He snatches the instruction book off Mickey "Give me the manual. I'll be back in half an hour."

He rapidly heads off down the street and jumps into his car.

Joby wanders out of the club in time to see Digger trotting away "Where's he off?"

"He's discovered that a gas BBQ actually needs gas."

Joby looks at his watch "Well he'd better hurry up it's 10:15 already. People are due to start turning up at noon."

"He'll be fine, don't worry. He's only gone to the DIY place"

Joby puts his arm around Mickey's shoulders "Ah, how sweet. You've not known him as long as me, have you?

*If I get lost along the way to meet you*
*If i'm more than a little late*
*If I get caught up in circles chasing my own tail*
*If I trip up and fail you*
*If i let you down*
*If i let you down*

\* \* \*

Digger has negotiated his way through the Sunday morning traffic and is now at the DIY store. Having run around like a headless chicken for ten minutes he has succumbed and decided to seek out an assistant. The lad, a boy of questionable skin management ponders Digger's request and delivers his response.

"All gorn mate. It's the weather. Should have some in Wednesday though."

He turns to walk away. Digger grabs his arm "That's no good, it's an emergency, you must have some! I have a congregation arriving in an hour."

The teenager stares blankly back "You could try that new place."

"New place? What new place? Where the hell is that?"

"Down by the Rye."

Digger realises he is on a loser here "Shit that's miles away. Ok thanks."

He sprints through the door and to the car. Heading back into Wycombe he arrives at the new outlet and breathlessly jogs in and after a few minutes breathlessly jogs out. Empty handed.

"Spotty oik!"

He speeds off to a suggested garden centre in the Bucks countryside with dread in his heart and his confidence sinking.

* * *

Back at the club Joby is going over the day's menu with Mickey "So young Michael what culinary goodies have you got for us?"

Mickey is resplendent in his pristine pinny "Well taking on board the Gospel theme, we have the Halleluiah Burger, that comes with onions and a choice of mustard or ketchup. The Save My Soul sausage bap and, for the more adventurous, the Oh My God Caribbean chicken, which is hot, believe me. Reverand Ness gave me his Mum's recipe."

Joby rubs his hands together "Excellent. You'll make someone a lovely wife some day."

He looks up the street "Of course all we need now is to get this going." He pats the BBQ "It's ten past eleven already. He must be back soon surely."

Joby pulls his mobile out and starts dialling "I'll call him. It's ringing. -Digger where the hell are you? - Where's that? - Really? Well I never knew they had a garden centre there." He holds the phone from his ear as loud shouting can be heard across the ether "So have you got one? - Well stop tarting about and hurry up."

\* \* \*

In the depths of Bucks, a frantic Digger jams his phone back into his pocket and continues to drag a reluctant trolley weighed down by a large gas cylinder. After several attempts he successfully negotiates a path around the potting plants and comes to a grinding halt at the cashier's desk.

"Thanks very much you've saved my life."

A pretty young lady in a logo emblazoned tracksuit sits behind the till "You were lucky we had that one lying around. Been a big run on them."

"You're telling me."

Digger gratefully pays with his credit card praying that Pandora hasn't gone over the limit.

"Thanks again. "He looks at his watch and sees it is 11:25 "Bloody hell this is going to be close."

He grabs the trolley and drags it heavily and slowly across the gravel car park, past the stone ornaments, the buddhas and the fencing panels, around the 2 for 1 compost sacks to where a helpful assistant assists him in loading the gas cylinder into the boot. With a spin of the wheels, a shower of dust and a toot of thanks he heads back towards town.

\* \* \*

Joby and Mickey pace up and down in the street outside the club. They hear Digger before they see him as the car screeches around the corner and skids to a halt in front of them.

Joby throws his arms in the air in annoyance as Digger jumps out and runs to the rear of the car ignoring his partner's ranting. He fretfully calls to the chunterring Joby as he tries to unload the cylinder.

"Bloody hell. Here we are, take it, weighs a ton. If you knew where I have been. Places I didn't know even existed."

Joby doesn't care "Save the sob story till later. Let's get this thing fired up"

Between them Joby and Mickey manouver and stand the cylinder at the rear of the BBQ. Mickey attaches the appropriate hoses. "There we go. Piece of cake. Don't know what the fuss is all about." He looks at the panting Digger "You alright boss?"

Digger meanwhile is leaning forward with his hands on his knees, exhausted from his unexpected exercise. Normally, turning the pages of the Mail on Sunday is the only work out he gets at the weekend.

Joby dismissively stares at him shaking his head "He's fine. Here put a t-shirt on."

"Yeah, yeah I'm - gasp - fine. Mickey, get the charcoal on, pile it up and get that thing blazing. Start cooking in about 10 minutes, ok? I'll send Donna out to help."

Mickey is sceptical "Are you sure that's how it works?"

Digger is in no mood for arguments "Just do it."

Mickey shrugs "Ok if you say so."

Joby has little sympathy "Come on let's just make sure everything inside is ready. Shake a leg." He ushers a red-faced Digger into the club for the last-minute checks.

* * *

As predicted, around noon the "congregation" begins to arrive. A mixture of club regulars in jeans and t-shirts and newcomers from the mission in their Sunday best. All are greeted by Joby, Pandora and Digger, resplendent in Easily Led t-shirts who escort them to tables. The club is a hive of activity and chatter, as people get their drinks then form a queue for food. The BBQ is in full flow with smoke billowing and the tempting smell of food filling the air. Mickey and Donna are fighting to keep up with the early demand but it doesn't stop Donna's eye being caught by the sight of Charlie staring at them, as he cuts up some strips of material.

Donna wipes her hands on her apron and nods his way "Mickey what do you think he's up to?"

Mickey doesn't even look up as he struggles to cope "No idea. I have enough problems with the Oh My God Chicken. Running a bit low. Keep cooking Donna. Save My Soul sir? Onions with that?"

A mini bus pulls up and the choir, Safiya and Tony disembark. A selection of shapes, sizes and ages, a mixture of a few handsome young men and women all smiles and all dressed in black. They file past the BBQ giving complimentary oohs and ahhs and into the club, to congregate. Safiya quickly nips through the smoke to plant a kiss on Mickey's cheek before joining her colleagues. This somehow manages to make him go even redder and encourages him to attack a burning sausage with added endeavour.

Tony embraces the dishevelled Donna as Digger comes out to greet them.

"Tony welcome. All your guys here?"

Tony drapes an arm around Digger as they enter "Indeed we are all here and ready to sing." He looks around "And where is Pandora. She is my main reason for being here you know!"

Digger chuckles "Naturally. Oh, she's around somewhere. Oh yes, over there behind the bar."

Digger goes to move through the choir members but before he can escape, he is grabbed and kissed by a selection of the ladies "Oh - Thank you – Yes - Hello, hello, welcome, lovely to see you too. – Ouch, you'll never go to heaven madam. Look, get some food and make yourselves at home."

The Reverend Tony looks around nodding appreciatively "Great turn out guys. Well done Digger. We'll grab a bite and then we'll be ready."

He spies Joby across the floor and waves. Joby indicates in hectic semaphore that he will catch him later.

The choir take turns to fill their plates and sit on the edge of the stage. Tony circulates around the club shaking hands with people, looking for converts and eventually reaches a leather clad Pandora who is serving behind the bar. She comes around and gives Tony a big hug. He steps back and looks her up and down.

"Looking great Pandora. Love the outfit."

"Oh, stop it. You are such a naughty man."

Joby catches up with them and slaps Tony on the back

"Hey big man put her down you can't afford her. You know I can't remember when I was this excited, it's going to be fantastic. I am literally having trouble breathing."

Tony laughs showing a mouth full of brilliant white teeth "That's the smoke from the BBQ probably. That thing is really going now."

And so, it is time. The choir take to the stage where the band is ready and waiting as Digger steps up to the microphone "Brothers and sisters. A very warm welcome to the first ever Church of the Easily Led Sunday Gospel lunch."

Cheers and applause and at least one halleluiah.

He continues "We are delighted so many of our easily led members could make it today and why wouldn't you, being …. easily led. Just to let you know there are some fabulous t-shirts and CD's available at the bar so don't be stingy investing your money and, of course, the BBQ is still going outside if you haven't eaten yet. Apparently, the food is great so don't be shy."

Joby with a huge smile on his face joins Pandora behind the bar under the picture of Ken. He feels he is going to burst with anticipation and excitement.

Joby had never shied away from Gospel music unlike many people who feel uncomfortable because of the religious roots and who feel like intruders interloping into a special club. To him it's all about the music and the feeling. In truth Gospel varies in style and flavour. Certain performers limit themselves to appearing in religious contexts only, whilst others have performed both secular and religious music and it is into this category that Tony's choir falls. They just do the lot. Joby feels it's all about the passion and the sound. It's music that does something to the soul of believers, non believers and The Easily Led alike.

On the stage Digger continues "So without further ado please welcome the Blues Hole Band with the very, very wonderful Church of the Easily Led choir."

And so, it starts. Tony stands facing his choir and holds his hands ready. The expectancy throughout the bar is electric. The keyboard gurgles out a cheesy rolling gospel organ sound, Tony's hands flash and the choir launch into a searing version of The Winans – All you ever been was Good. They rock the house then they soothe the house. People can't sit still as they clap and whoop. And so it goes. There are cries from the audience as the music rises and falls, the choruses rolling on and on in a crescendo of human joy. They do modern gospel; they do traditional favourites.

Joby working behind the bar feels a tear trickle down his cheek especially when he hears them sing The Temptations – Papa was a rolling stone, his Dad's favourite. The picture of Ken above him sits like a hairy religious icon benignly looking down. The Blues Hole Band excel themselves with their sympathetic playing, quiet here, rocking there, Ben's keyboard rippling along. A perfect set. And it seems that as soon as it starts, it ends. The audience are on their feet, the choir are hugging anyone within hugging distance. Digger is lost in the commotion until Pandora advances to drag him free so he can breathlessly mount the stage. Joby realises he's also been holding his breath and that he can now breathe again.

Digger is beaming "How about that? Please put your hands together for the wonderful Church of the Easily Led Choir and the Blues Hole Band."

The "congregation" cheer to the rafters as the choir wave and head for the doors.

Digger wraps it up "Don't forget t-shirts and cd's are available at the bar and remember the choir will be back in two week's time so get your tickets now and tell all your friends. We hope you've had a wonderful time. Get home safely."

Joby is selling merchandise by the bucket load. A beaming Tony leans across to shake hands with his old friend.

"Joby that was great. They amazed even me. What was in those burgers?"

Joby laughs "Secret recipe. I absolutely loved it Tone. It was fantastic. Don't get any ideas about converting me though, too long in the tooth."

Tony wags a finger at him "Never too late Joseph"

Joby shakes his head" Haven't been called that in a long time Tony."

Digger having said his goodbyes joins them "Nice one chaps. Thanks Tone it was brilliant. Listen, I have to go and sort the BBQ out so I'll say bye. Speak later, eh?"

"Sure. I've got to go as well so peace be with you oh leaders of the easily led. Let's speak in the week."

Joby comes round the bar and they walk to the door. Tony joins his flock on the mini bus and Joby waves a fond farewell.

As Pandora, Safiya and Donna start to tidy up the boys attempt to get the BBQ inside. Digger and Mickey are fighting with the beast.

Digger is disdainful of Mickey's efforts "I thought you were supposed to be strong Mr. Muscle. Black belt my arse."

Mickey, who seems to be doing most of the work, responds "I've been slogging over a hot stove all day. It's you, you wimp, lift it up. Shit, it's bloody hot this end. Should'nt we leave it outside?"

"What and have it nicked? No way Jose."

After much huffing and puffing and several helpful suggestions from Joby they manoeuvre the BBQ through the club.

Digger shakes his arms to relieve the strain "Stick it down here behind the bar out of the way."

More huffing and the BBQ is dragged into place.

Joby takes up a broom to start sweeping the floor "What a brilliant day. Pandora how much did we take?

Pandora is counting the takings and smiling. "Don't know yet but it's very good. Religion pays well it seems."

They tidy and sort, wash the glasses and stack chairs so by six o'clock the club is in a state where they all can leave.

Joby locks the door as the gang congregate outside. He kisses Pandora and Safiya on the cheek and shakes Mickey's hand.

"Thanks everyone it's been a great day."

Over the road Charlie is still wandering about outside the garage glowering across at them.

Joby whispers in Digger's ear and nods "What's he up to?"

Digger slyly takes a peek "No idea mate. Whatever it is it's no good, I'm sure. Hey we're off, speak tomorrow, ok?"

"Yeah sure. Great day, and as an added bonus you found a lost garden centre and made a new friend at the DIY store. Well done."

"Very funny. See ya later. Oh, I'll pick the BBQ up in the morning."

"Ok mate. Bye Pandora, bye Mickey, great work Safiya. Come on Donna lets hit the trail."

They walk off into the sunset Joby whistling gospel tunes and Donna holding on to his arm. Life was great.

*I have had some hardships*
*Plenty of sweat across my brow*
*All you ever been was good*
*And if they ask me to testify*
*A thousand years from now*
*I'd say all you ever been was good*

# Chapter 14

Joby is dreaming about something involving a penguin, a giant clown on a bicycle and balloons when his sleep is shattered by the ringtone of his mobile laying on the bedside table. He throws an arm over to grab it, sees the radio alarm registers 1:30am and grumpily leans up on one elbow gruffly mumbling into the hand set.

"Hello. This had better be good."

An unknown voice "Mr. Black?"

"Yeah, who is this?"

Unknown voice "Mr. Black this is Wycombe Fire Station. It's your premises in Evergreen Street sir, a fire has broken out and I suggest you attend immediately."

"What? Is that you Digger you wanker, have you been on the piss, is this a joke?"

The unknown voice is assertive "I can assure you sir this is no joke. We have managed to contain the blaze but obviously there is considerable damage. Fortunately for you we received an anonymous call from a member of the public or it would have been much worse."

Joby is suddenly wide awake "Oh shit! Ok thanks I'm on my way. Oh, and sorry about the wanker bit."

He ends the call and leaps out of bed, turning lights on and clambering into his jeans.

Hopping on one leg "No! No! No! Bastards. Donna wake up, the club's on fire. I have to get down there. I'll call Digger."

Donna takes off her eyemask and sits up "What? A fire? How did that happen?"

Joby has no mind for pleasantries "How the hell should I know, but that Charlie was hanging around earlier looking suspicious. He's number one on the list."

"He wouldn't do that, would he?"

Joby is pulling on a jumper and some shoes "Well I wouldn't put it past him. I'll know more when I get there. Someone called the Fire Brigade thank god."

Donna slides out of bed and into her dressing gown "That at least was lucky. Listen you go and I'll follow in a little while. Shall I call anyone else?"

Joby grabs his mobile and coat and heads out of the door "No, I'll do it on the way."

Running out of the door he dials and a sleepy voice answers.

"Digger! - Digger wake up! It's me - Joby - listen the club's on fire so get your arse down there now - Does it sound like a sodding joke - well tough you'll have to rekindle the passion later - no I have no idea, I'll meet you there."

*Pick up any morning paper*
*Turn on the 6 o'clock news*
*The devil's been so busy lately*
*That even God must get the blues*

\* \* \*

Joby can smell the smoke long before he sees it. He rounds the corner to see two fire appliances. their lights like a carnival, and a host of firemen milling outside the smoking doors of the club. A number of hoses are laid out on the road like glistening tape worms and there is water everywhere. Joby breathlessly runs up to the nearest fireman.

"Joby Black, joint owner. Shit what a mess, what a fucking mess. Any news?"

The firefighter is sympathetic "Well sir it could have been worse. Fortunately, we got here pretty quick. We've put the main fire out but we can't enter the building yet."

"Thank god for that. Any idea what caused it? Could it have been arson?"

The firefighter shrugs his shoulders "Like I said sir, too early to say. In a few hours, when it's light, we can have a better look."

He leaves Joby and goes about his work. Joby stands and stares in bemusement, not knowing what feelings were going around his head. Digger's car pulls up at the end of the street and he trots down to join Joby. He has a pair of oven gloves on his hands.

He waves his mittened hands ""Oh my god what a mess. What caused it?"

Joby stares at his buddy "What on earth are you wearing?"

Digger looks at his hands "Oh these. Just in case I had to handle anything hot. First thing I could grab."

Joby explains "The boys here don't know what caused it yet. But I saw that bastard Charlie hanging around all afternoon. My money's on him. Some warped retribution for Ken's fun and games."

Digger waves his hands about like a demented Andy Pandy "Surely he wouldn't stoop to this. That's fucking criminal."

Joby has a resigned look "Don't think he worries too much about the criminal element of it. We'll find out more when it gets light. I can't believe that all our hard work is ruined."

He stops a passing fireman "Anything we can do to help officer?

"Not really sir. Best you can do is to keep out of the way or go home."

Digger is affronted "Go home? I just got here. No way. I'm staying right here. Too much money invested just to clear off."

Joby agrees "Me too."

"Ok guys but don't be a nuisance. We'll do our best to be as careful as we can inside. There's some coffee over there so help yourselves."

The guys move away, grab some coffee and sit on the kerb. A pall of misery hangs over them. Coffee cup between his feet Joby has his head in his hands "After all we've been through, then this. Someone up there just really hates me."

Digger tries to be positive "Listen it might not be that bad. It might just look worse than it is. Let's see in a few hours, eh?"

Joby slowly lowers his hands and raises his head to face his best friend.

"Digger god bless you. It's been torched and had a million gallons of water sluiced through it. Believe me it ain't going to be a dustpan and brush job. I tell you; this is it for me. All those years of failing and fucking up, I really thought for once I'd done something right. I really, really tried."

He sniffles back a tear "I've never worked so hard for so long in my life. But no ... shit on from a great height yet again. What's the point? Why do the bastards always win? Digger I never hurt anyone, ever. It's just not fair." He bursts into tears.

Digger makes a vain attempt to put his arm around the sobbing Joby but the oven gloves get in the way, so together they sit forlornly as the work to save their livelihood goes on around them.

*Somebody pick up my pieces I'm scattered everywhere*
*And put me back together And put me way over there*
*Take me out of contention I surrender my crown*
*So somebody pick up my pieces*
*It's just me comin' down*

\* \* \*

At least, when it was dark, they couldn't see the whole misery of the situation but as dawn breaks the full extent of the damage slowly becomes apparent. The boys had resigned themselves to the cold facts that The Blues Hole, as they knew it, was no more. Pandora and Donna had arrived and were comforting their respective partners and trying to be positive. Then around 7:30 am Charlie arrives to unlock his premises. Joby sees him and races across the road to confront him.

"Hey you! Look what you've done to my club you bastard."

Charlie stops unlocking and turns to face his accuser "What are you talking about?"

Joby is incensed and jostles Charlie at the door "You know very well what I'm talking about. I saw you yesterday, hanging around with that petrol can looking furtive and you've got a motive. Look at my fucking club!"

Charlie pushes him away and opens the garage door "You're bloody mad you are. So, you reckon cos I have a petrol can then

I set fire to your dump over there. Well look around. If you haven't noticed this is a garage. We use petrol all the time."

He points inside the door to several green cans sitting on the floor

"Was it one of them?"

"Yeah. That's it! And you had a load of bottles and rags. You arsonist!"

Joby pushes past Charlie and grabs a can. Its heavier than he thought it would be.

Charlie stares at him "Well I think if you have a look you'll see that can is still full up. They all are."

Joby takes the top off a couple and sure enough they are full to the brim.

Charlie continues "And as for the bottles well my missus makes me recycle them down the end of the street. Pain in the arse. I'd sling 'em but she's all into this recycling bollocks. Do you see any here now? "

Joby frowns and looks around. He doesn't see any.

"If ya want I'll take you down the end and show you. I stacked em by the bin cos it was full. And as for rags. We use loads to clean the engines, wipe things down. There they are."

He points to a pile on a bench. Then sarcastically "You might need some by the look of it. Help yourselves."

He throws some at Joby "So that's that theory out the window."

He pushes Joby outside "Listen, I didn't set fire to your club knobhead. What I want is the money you owe me and with your club closed, what chance will I have of ever seeing it, eh? Think about that why don't you. Now sod off."

He slams the door in their faces. They stand in silence until Digger chips in. "He could be right Joby."

Joby is less certain "Well I'm not convinced. We'll soon see when the boys go in."

He opens the Garage door and shouts inside "Don't you go anywhere Charlie. This isn't over."

Charlie shouts back from the office "I don't plan too. Unlike you I work for a living. Got a big job to finish. Been on it all weekend. So why don't you bugger off and let me get on with it."

He turns his back and slams the office door leaving Joby and Digger to wander back across the road to where the Fire chief is standing talking to a colleague.

Joby approaches them "Any idea when we can go in?"

The firechief turns "We'll have a look in a few minutes. Oh, by the way I found the phone number that called this in. Mobile number it was. Registered to a Mr K. Loveloss. Believe me you need to find him and thank him. Here's the number."

Joby takes it with a wan smile "Thanks I'll call him a bit later. Wonder what he was doing round here that time of night? Name doesn't ring a bell. Whatever, he's a hero."

Mickey has arrived and the five of them stand in a sad lonely huddle. Donna is concerned about Joby. "Are you alright baby?"

He looks at her in amazement "Alright? No, I'm not alright Donna. Why would you think I'd be alright? This is the final nail as far as I'm concerned."

She tries to be positive "Don't worry it will all be fine. The insurance will cover it. You did pay the insurance, didn't you?"

"Of course we did, but that'll take months. You know what they're like. By the time they try and wriggle out of paying, and then finally cough up something, we'll be back to square one and broke. You remember the fuss we had over that lost luggage. Bunch of shysters."

She gives him a little shake "Come on Joby we've been through worse."

Joby sighs and pulls away "Actually Donna I don't think we have."

A fireman comes over "We're just about to go in but you guys need to stay back, ok?"

After a few minutes he is back out.

Joby is impatient "What did you find? Is it bad? How did it start?"

The fireman takes his breathing apparatus off "Hang on sir, one question at a time. The damage is fairly extensive at this near end of the club where the bar and toilet area are. The far end is smoke damaged but not too bad. Good job we got here quickly. How did it start? Well, it looks like the source of the fire is situated in the bar area but my colleague is still in there."

Digger is puzzled "The bar area? Why would it start there? "

Joby has his theories "Charlie probably thought the spirits would catch alight and cause more damage."

The second fireman comes out carrying Ken's guitar "This was on the wall in the toilet but sorry it seems to have been damaged. Very strange, cos the rest of the toilet was totally untouched,"

Digger takes it off of him "Thanks. No that's how it's supposed to look. How ironic, a burnt guitar is about the only thing that wasn't burnt."

Joby can't believe it" Sodding typical."

The Fireman explains "It seems your toilet door acted as a fire shield. Piece of luck that."

Joby "This thing has a charmed life. I'll stick it in the car."

The fireman then delivers a chilling message "Oh and there was something behind the bar which, if I didn't know better, I'd say was a BBQ or a grill or something. Hard to tell as it's all mangled but at a rough guess I would say it's around there that the fire could have started."

He wanders off. Digger pulls Joby to one side and whispers in his ear.

"That can't be I turned it off. No, honestly I did. It was definitely turned off. The gas had run out so it couldn't have been left on."

Joby thinks about this news and gets a bad feeling "And the charcoal? Did you empty that ton of hot embers out of it?"

Digger frowns, turns and asks Mickey "Did you empty the hot charcoal out of it?

Mickey is infuriated "Me? No, you said you'd sort it out today. I just helped carry it in. Burnt my hands, it was bloody hot. "

Joby throws his hands up in the air in exasperation" Oh for fu - You dopey pair of ...!"

He pulls away and finds the fireman.

"Was there any sign of a petrol bomb?"

The fireman is puzzled at this "Petrol bomb? No sir we'd tell that almost straight away by the smell. Absolutely not. I would say, almost certainly, that the fire started in the bar area."

The fireman goes about his work as Digger protests his innocence to anyone who would listen.

"I didn't know. I never use the BBQ. Pandora, tell them I never touch it."

Pandora is stood with her arms folded staring at him with a deep scowl on her face "Digger that was stupid, where vas your brain."

Mickey butts in "I just carried it in, nothing to do with me Joby."

Joby is beside himself "And there I was accusing Charlie of terrorism! You pissing idiots!" He paces around "I thought at least there was one person in this world I could trust but no. You and" He points the guitar towards Mickey "grasshopper there have cost us everything. Please tell me you didn't do anything else stupid, cos you were messing about behind the bar for ages "

Digger thinks "No of course not. All I did was hang some tea towels up to dry."

"Anywhere near the BBQ by any chance?"

Digger is very sheepish "Might have been."

"How near?"

"Quite near."

"How fucking near is quite near?"

"On the lid."

Joby can't take any more "Oh for god's sake! Just leave me alone both of you, don't talk to me."

Guitar in hand he stomps to the end of the street where his car is parked. Having deposited it in the boot he sits on the kerb, a sad lonely figure, the troubles of the world weighing down on his slumped shoulders.

*Won't you talk to me about your problems*
*Tell me all about your ways*
*Sometimes I feel like a helpless child*
*Won't you help me through these rock bottom days*

Donna is trying to calm things down.

"Mickey it wasn't your fault, Digger don't worry he'll come round. They don't know for certain it was the BBQ. Even if it was, it was an accident, I'm sure. Listen we need to contact the insurance people. Perhaps you could do that Pandora."

Pandora isn't so sympathetic.

She gestures at them "You two are a pair of Achterlijke."

She puts an admonishing hand up "Don't ask Digger just accept you are! Leave the insurance people to me Donna. I'll just tell them the basics, need to know basis, say no more."

"Thanks Pandora." She indicates down the street "Digger go and talk to him. He's just upset. Don't forget how much he loves running the club with you."

Digger nods and slowly walks down to where Joby is sat head in hands. He sits down on the kerb next to him.

"Are you ok?"

Joby slowly looks up "Ok? Ok? Why is everyone asking if I'm ok? Of course I'm not fucking ok. You've just burnt our club down. Only thing that came out unscathed was that pissing guitar, which was already fucking burnt!"

"Joby, they aren't certain it was the BBQ. All we know is that it wasn't Charlie."

Joby gives an ironic snort "Digger you know it was the BBQ and I know it was the BBQ. And now we have the job of convincing the insurance people it wasn't the BBQ. We are buggered with a capital B! I need to think."

He puts his head back in his hands momentarily then up again. "We worked so hard. I worked so hard for the first time in my life and I still lost out."

Head back down. Head back up. His face suddenly very tired. "I should ring that number and see who called the fire brigade and thank them at least. Then I'd better go and apologise to Charlie and then decide what we say to the insurance people."

He stands and leaves Digger. Taking out his phone he walks back towards the club, reading and dialling the number he'd been given. It rings a few times and a gruff voice answers.

"Yes?"

"Hello is that Mr. Loveloss?"

"Yeah."

"Mr. Loveloss my name is Joby Black. I'm just calling to thank you for contacting the fire service last night and saving my club from complete ruin. If there is anything I can ever do for you just let me know."

"Yeah, you can give me the thirty grand you owe me."

Joby spins round and sees Charlie stood at the garage door, phone to his ear.

Joby is agape "You!"

He ends the call and goes over to face Charlie.

"What the fu..Why didn't you tell us you'd called the fire brigade?"

Charlie growls at him "What, and miss all the fun. No way. You're even more obliged to me now."

"But what on earth were you doing here that late?"

"I told you I was working. Unlike you I have a reputation to maintain."

Joby shakes his head "Charlie, I owe you an apology. We all owe you an apology."

"Shove your apology. What you owe me is my money and the chances of me getting that now look even more remote. Should have let it burn."

Joby tries to explain "But when your boys caused all that trouble, we naturally thought you were out for revenge."

"The boys were just looking out for their father. I didn't ask them to do anything. They're just high spirited."

Joby holds his hands out "What can I say apart from sorry."

He suddenly thinks "Hey this number is registered to a K. Loveloss"

"That's me. Kimberley Loveloss."

"But you're called Charlie."

He points to the dirt covered sign above the door which reads KCL Motors

"My middle name. Would you want to be called Kimberley? What sort of stupid name is that to give a boy. Poof's name."

"Yeah, I see your point."

"Now clear off so I can get on with my work."

He turns, leaving Joby stood alone. Joby stands there a minute and then goes slowly back across the road to join the others.

Digger is obviously curious "What happened there?"

Joby is grudgingly talking to his friend again. "Turns out that not only did Charlie not set fire to the club, but he was our guardian angel. He called the fire brigade."

"Never! Why didn't he say something the sick sod?"

"Warped sense of humour. Guess he didn't think it important. I apologised. Felt about 2 feet tall. Not been a good day so far."

Joby shoves his hands in his pockets "He says he still wants his money but of course now he doesn't have any chance of that. Seems we all lose."

Digger tries to explain "Listen I ….."

Joby slowly places a placating arm around Digger's shoulders "Digger listen. I was thinking sat down there on my own. Last night you were an irresponsible tosser, a fuckwit of the first order, a wanker, a knob, totally stupid, no doubt about that, an absolute brainless dimwit. No court in the land would convict me if I beat you to death with that shit guitar, right here in the middle of the street."

Digger looks downcast as Joby continues.

"But over the years how many times has that been me and not you?"

Digger sulkily "A few I guess."

"Digger we both know it's been more than a few. You were always there for me. And how many times have you bailed me out, leant me money and never got paid back?"

Digger perking up "More than a few. Are you paying it all back?"

Joby turns to face him "Ah, no. The way I see it is this - I guess you're owed one big one. And this is it. And to be honest nothing I say or do, will compare in any way, shape or form to the bollocking Pandora is going to give you when you get home. Good luck there by the way."

He ruffles Digger's hair "Come on, let's see what we can salvage before we devise a plan to get some money back."

*You may forgive, but you never forget*
*And you tell everybody you got no regrets*
*You take your chances and sometimes you lose*
*And you need someone to get you over the blues*

# Chapter 15

After a further couple of hours, they were allowed into the club for a brief period. No one wanted to be first and so Pandora led the way followed by the other three. As they stepped through the remains of the door, they were faced with a scene that ranged from hell at one end, to relative (apart from serious smoke damage) normality at the other. The walls were black with soot, the smell of damp cremation was overpowering and the bar area was totally destroyed. Indeterminate lumps of what could be metal lay on the floor where the bar once stood. Twisted optics hung from the wall, nothing remained of Ken's picture. At the far end of the club the stage, tables and chairs remained strangely intact, water glistening across the floor. It was a club of two halves.

Joby gingerly splashed across the wet, ash strewn floor to the toilets and pushed opened the heavy door. Inside, it was as if nothing had ever happened. He made a mental note to give John a bonus, then realised that actually he now had no money, so a thank you would have to do. There were still some areas that were smoking and water dripped everywhere, so they decided to cut the visit short and to adjourn to Digger's to gather their thoughts.

Back at Chez Jones, Donna and the boys are sat around the kitchen table. The smell of smoke hung around them so Pandora has opened all the windows and is busy lighting aromatherapy candles all over the house.

Digger swigs from his coffee cup "How strange was that guitar. I can't believe that. That's just spooky."

Joby shakes his head in annoyance "Bloody jinx. It can stay in the boot. I'm going to dump it. Next time I go to High Heavens that's going with me."

Digger tries to convince him otherwise "Maybe you should keep it. I think it's an omen, you know Phoenix out of the fire and all that. Up to you of course."

He dunks a biscuit "Pandora just called the insurance company and they're sending an assessor down. We need to decide what we are going to say to them."

Pandora has finished fumigating and joins them "Should be here 10 a.m tomorrow, so you'd better have a good story. Me, I'd just play the dode kat." She looks at their blank faces "Dead cat, dutch saying."

Joby has decided that a positive front is the one to take in this, his worst of days. He has a plan "What we say is nothing. We have no idea what caused it. Yes, there was a BBQ in there but it was empty. No, no idea officer. I have decided I am not being beaten by this."

Digger cottons on quick "Basically lie then."

Joby is insulted "No not at all. Just don't tell them all the facts. We actually have no idea if the BBQ caused the fire, so let's not put any thoughts in their heads, ok? Let them work it out. That's what they're paid for."

Digger dunks "Mmm, Suppose so."

Donna is not convinced "Joby are you sure that's a good idea."

Joby is firm "What? We pay enough premiums and I guarantee they will try and wriggle out, whatever the truth is, so we are not digging a hole for ourselves. We absolutely don't know what started the fire and that's it. We are fronting this out."

Joby's mobile rings and stops any further arguments.

"Hello - oh Mr.Williams how are you ? - Oh you've heard - yes you could say a bit of trouble at the club - A fire yes - no all under control now - Not good no - they're fine thanks - Ken's guitar? Well amazingly it was about the only thing to get out unscathed, not a scratch, not that you'd notice of course. Put it down to British workmanship - good old John and his bog door - It's in the car at present. I'm taking it up the dump later. Bloody thing's jinxed."

At this final announcement there is a large amount of ranting down the phone. Joby pulls a pained face and holds the phone away from his ear. Eventually the shouting stops.

"Ok, Ok, Calm down, you'll have a bleeding heart attack - Yes I understand. I won't do anything - I promise - Ok I'll be there at three, bye."

Digger has been watching his friend "What did he want?"

"Well, he'd heard about the fire and wanted to know if Ken's guitar was ok. Didn't care about me or you of course. I said it was fine and then he went ballistic when I said I was going to dump it cos it's jinxed." He points at his mobile "He used words no solicitor should know and insisted, yes insisted, he wants to see me this afternoon. Digger you're coming of course, sounds like I'll need a bodyguard."

"I'm your man. I've been exercising getting in shape lately."

"Mmm, I guess round is a shape. What is it with Williams and that guitar? If he wants it that badly he can have it."

Joby's mobile squawks again "Bloody hell. Hello – oh hi Safiya - we're all fine thanks, well as fine as can be - really?

that's good, I cant wait to see it - I bet you're excited - Yeah, lets get together - I'll call you, might be tomorrow though - ok bye for now."

He rings off and turns to Digger "Safiya has got that picture for us to look at."

Pandora leaps in "What picture is that Digger? Is this another secret you are keeping from me?"

Digger is dismissive "Oh, she just thinks we might know a relative of hers from some years ago that's all. Nothing to worry about."

Digger finishes his coffee as Joby announces with a wink towards his friend "Apparently, she doesn't recognise <u>anyone</u> in the picture Digger. The mystery remains."

Theres a crash and loud coughing as Digger drops his cup. Pandora rushes to clear it up. Sweeping around Digger's feet she berates him "Digger you are so clumsy today. First you burn the club and now even worse you break my best china. I must take you to the doctors. You have the dropsy."

The coughing stops as Digger enquires haltingly "So, she didn't recognise anyone, at all?"

Joby is smiling at his friend's relief "Well apart from her Mum, no. Any more coffee going Pandora, then we'd better clean up and go and see what dear Mr. Williams wants."

*Just another pain,*
*really it hurts so bad*
*Just another pain,*
*really it hurts so bad*
*Got the funniest feelin',*
*a man most ever had*

The boy's have accepted that the fate of the club is out of their hands. At the solicitors Joby is ensconced on the settee perusing another aged magazine. Digger nonchalantly leans on the wall next to him. He has been a new man since the revelation about the photograph and in the car the boys had been throwing names of suspects around. They had agreed that it could have been anyone. Joby quietly turns pages until he stops at an interesting article.

"Tits like coconuts apparently."

Digger perks up "Who has, Carol Vordermann?"

"No! Tits, birds, like, as in eat, coconuts. Well, that's what it says here. I've always just put out breadcrumbs. Oh, and guess what Britain's favourite hobby for the elderly was in 2002."

Digger ponders for a few moments shaking his head "Was it dogging?"

"What? No of course it wasn't dogging. It's surfing the web. Why would it be dogging? What goes on in that head?"

"Just a thought. Outdoor pursuit. I must have told you about my Aunty Barbara's experience in Penn Woods"

Joby throws the magazine down "Many times. What's keeping him?"

He calls over to the receptionist "Excuse me, we had an appointment at three and its quarter past. Can you just let his nibs know we're here. Again!"

The receptionist looks up and haughtily replies "Mr. Williams knows you are here sir but I will just remind him."

She dials and shouting can be heard through the office door.

She replaces the phone and politely addresses them "He says he'll be right with you sir."

Digger pulls a face "He sounds happy."

"He hasn't had his club burnt down. Then he'd have something to moan about. Fuck him I say."

The reception phone buzzes "He'll see you now sir."

Joby is up and heading towards the corner office "About time too. Thanks."

They enter to see Mr Williams sat behind his desk. He doesn't look happy as he points to two chairs.

"Sit."

They obediently sit.

Joby "Good afternoon Mr. Williams, nice to see you, at last."

Mr. Williams dispenses with niceties "Where's the guitar?"

Joby puts his hands up in exasperation "In the boot of my car. What is it about this sodding guitar that gets you so hot under the collar? It's a piece of junk for christ's sake. Of all the things that could have burnt it had to be the one thing that survived. So, tell me now, what's so special about it?"

Mr. Williams calms down and slowly leans forward his hands folded on the desk.

"Joby, I want you to listen very carefully to what I am about to say. As your Uncle's executor, he had me sworn to secrecy and I was only to tell you what I am going to tell you, in the event of a dire emergency. I guess today is that day. So please don't interrupt. OK?

"Ok"

Mr. Williams continues in a low voice "Your uncle was, despite all his other failings, and he had a few, a very astute man when it came to the music business and he knew more about rock history and memorabilia than anyone I knew."

He leans back "He won that guitar in a poker game in Las Vegas. He was also a very good poker player by the way, years of practice on tour buses apparently."

A small smile "I digress. This one particular evening he was playing poker with some other musicians and was, as usual winning, much to the annoyance of the other participants. One gentleman in particular took it on himself to take on your Uncle, to break him. By the end of the session your uncle had won all his money and was owed a considerable amount on top. Still with me?"

Joby shrugs "So he was a gambler as well as a philanderer."

"Quite. Anyway, as I said your Uncle was a rock history aficionado and when, as part payment of the debt, this guy offered Ken an old guitar, your guitar Joby, he took up the offer." He leans forward again. "Why you may ask, it's just an old guitar, in your words, a piece of junk. Well, he took one look at it and knew straight away what it was and where it had come from. He told me he couldn't believe his eyes. He saw, unlike you, in technical guitar terms, that it was a right-handed Fender Stratocaster guitar, flipped and reverse strung, keeping the low E string on top, allowing a left-handed player to play a right-handed guitar."

Joby shrugs and pulls a so what face. Digger is enthralled.

Mr. Williams continues "And like all classic guitars it also had a serial number on the neck plate which, when Ken saw it, confirmed he had found the holy grail. It was a find in a million."

Now they are interested. Digger punches Joby on the arm "I said it was a Fender, you said it was crap."

"Because it looks crap. How was I supposed to know? Go on Mr. Williams."

"Thank you. Your uncle then did some final digging and confirmed as to the guitar being exactly what he thought it was. The previous owner, the bad loser, being a drummer of small brain had no idea, and like you, thought it was worthless."

He leans back. It's Joby's turn to lean forward "Ok. So, what is it?"

Mr. Williams pauses for effect "There was always a story, an unsubstantiated rumour some said, that during 1964 and 1965 when Jimi Hendrix played with Little Richard, he was quoted as saying that he wanted to do with his guitar what Little Richard did with his voice, namely set the world on fire. So, one night in early sixtyfive, at a private gig in a small club in LA, he did the next best thing. He burnt his guitar onstage, your guitar. Your piece of junk. That was in fact the first time he'd ever done it."

Joby still doesn't understand "So I have an ex-Jimi Hendrix guitar, but he burnt guitars all over the place if I remember correctly."

Mr. Williams smiles "I can see you still don't quite comprehend the magnitude of this. Well, actually no, he didn't burn as many as people think, probably no more than two, three at the most. But this is the most infamous. This is it. This is where it started. Number one. Hendrix soon left for the UK where he messed around for a few months finally emerging as the superstar we remember."

Silence reigns so he continues.

"This guitar is unique. Ken was a huge Hendrix fan, one of the biggest, and during the years he was in the US he did a massive amount of digging into this rumour, this myth. Like I said his holy grail. I guess you could say he was obsessed. He was convinced it existed. He searched and found people who had been there that night. He managed to collate all the registration records for Fender guitars so he could match up times and dates. Then, after years of searching, out of nowhere, there it was. Owned by a drummer who had no idea what he had. How he must have thought, or felt, when he first saw it is beyond me. I'm surprised he didn't have a heart attack there and then."

He stares at Joby "It's a one off, it's the original and it's yours Joby."

Joby sits staring wide-eyed and open mouthed. Mr. Williams waits, but no comments come so he carries on.

"Joby, your uncle wanted you to be something, to be a winner in life. You were so much like him that he was afraid if you were told straightaway, you'd just sell it, probably squander the proceeds and his wishes would have come to nothing. This was his insurance policy. Strange as it is, he was very proud of you Joby but he didn't trust you, so he instructed me keep an eye on both you and the guitar. Quite frankly you've been a bloody nightmare and when I heard about the fire well, I feared the worst."

Joby's mouth slams shut as the enormity of the situation hits him "I've had it hanging in the bog for christ's sake, on the wall over the pisser - why didn't you just tell me."

He shakes his head as if to clear it. Then a big thought hits him.

"Ok, if it's so special how much is it worth? Tuppence, ten quid, ten grand. Is this where you tell me it's worth squillions?"

"Sorry Joby this is real life not television"

Digger has been transfixed listening and suddenly remembers something.

"Wasn't one of these sold recently. Fetched a few hundred thousand."

Mr. Williams nods "Two hundred and eighty thousand pounds."

He ponders Joby's question "I would suggest you would get similar, maybe a bit more, say about three hundred thousand, even more in the right circumstances."

Joby's stress level lowers as a smile spreads over his face.

"Well, that's not bad at all, that's fantastic. That'll sort the club out at least and a good wack left over. Nice one Ken. In fact, bloody brilliant one Kenny boy. "

Then the enormity hits him as Joby leaps to his feet and heads for the door.

"Out the way I think I'm going to be sick"

*Girls, if you've got a rich man,*
*you'd better chain him to your side*
*Yes, if you've got a rich man,*
*you'd better chain him to your side*
*'Cause if he ever flags this train,*
*I'm sure going to let him ride*

They clean Joby up and after more discussions with his now favourite solicitor, a shaken and silent Joby is driven home by Digger.

* * *

Sat in Digger's lounge, Donna is gently mopping Joby's brow.

"Are you feeling better angel?

Joby thinks deeply "Feeling better? I feel brilliant Donna. Starving and empty, but brilliant. Sort of lighter all over."

Pandora nonchalantly stands over him looking down "So what did you do after you had chucked up your ontbijt all over the toilet floor?"

"Well, Digger raced down to the car, got the guitar and we put it in Mr. Williams' strong room for safe keeping."

Joby puts his hands over his eyes "I kept thinking about what could have happened and what if this and what if that. What if John hadn't fixed the bog door, what if it had fallen off the wall. What if I'd dumped it!"

Donna dabs some more "Well he did fix the door and it didn't fall off the wall, you didn't dump it and it didn't burn. Joby it's brilliant news. Well done."

Digger taps him on the knee "So what are you going to do now rich boy?"

"Wel, l I've asked Mr. Williams to look for a suitable buyer, maybe go to auction and when it's sold, we'll see what we have and make a decision then. One thing I do know is I am paying Charlie his thirty grand and I'm rebuilding that club."

He sits up and looks at Digger "Are you in with me Sparky or have you had enough?"

Digger's mouth opens like a guppy but Pandora speaks for both "Of course he is. I have never seen him so happy as when he is in that club. As we say in Holland - gelukkig als varken in shit. True Digger?

Digger frowns and shakes his head "My Dutch is a little bit sketchy but I'm guessing at what that means and yes I am as happy as a pig in you know what. However, let's not forget we have the insurance people to sort out. So, let's not all get over excited. The assessor is due tomorrow. "

Joby sits up "You're right Dig. Money or no money, we need to sort that out."

Pandora steps forward "You vant me to work on him. Mentally rough him up a bit?"

Joby raises a hand "Let's keep you in reserve angel shall we."

She frowns a disappointed frown and wanders into the kitchen taking Donna with her.

Joby leans towards Digger "And don't forget Safiya and her photo, but we can put that off until tomorrow as well."

Digger wrinkles his nose "That'll be interesting. I think. "

Joby waves a dismissive hand "It won't be you if what she said was true and if what you said was true. Two johnnies over a marshmallow? Nah. Seems our Myra, as well as being beautiful, was a bit of a raver. It'll be Keith or someone."

"Well let's hope so, otherwise I have a lot of explaining to do before I get beaten to a pulp by the Dutch middleweight champion. I'm in enough trouble already."

"Listen, Safiya would have said on the phone if she'd recognised you."

He ponders a second "Mind you, you did look different in those days. Very smooth with your long blond hair and your eyes of blue."

Digger lets out a big sigh "You're just not being a help here Joby."

The girls return with more tea. Joby takes a sip, grins and thinks of his empty stomach.

"It's been a hell of a day and I know that we shouldn't be celebrating, what with the club burning down but what do you say to a Chinese from Ho's. I'll pay, I think we can run to twenty quid."

> *I was waitin' in Rosie's Restaurant*
> *When the waiter came up and said, "What do you want?"*
> *I looked at the menu -- it looked so nice*
> *Till he said, "Let me give you some advice*
> *He said, "Spaghetti and potatoes got too much starch,*
> *Pork chops and sausage are bad for your heart.*
> *There's hormones in chicken and beef and veal.*
> *A bowl of ravioli is a dead man's meal."*

The following morning Joby and Digger reconvened outside the decimated club. They idly passed the time chatting, waiting for the insurance assessor to arrive. John had temporarily patched up the front door but the club has a desolate look and feel permeating from it. Joby has recovered from the shock of the revelations.

"Do you know what I learnt in Mr Williams' toilet yesterday?"

Digger shrugs "That toilet duck stinks?"

Joby kicks at some charred wood "No, but you're right it does. I learnt that you can keep vomiting long after you think you're finished. I don't remember when I last had half of what came out. My stomach must be like the tardis."

"Nice." Digger nods down the street "This could be our chappie."

Walking towards them is a short, rotund man wearing heavy round tortoiseshell glasses. He sports an orange anorak, woolly beanie hat and a duffle bag, with a clipboard firmly under his arm.

He approaches the boys "Mr. Black, Mr. Jones? Morning to you, lovely day, isn't it?"

Joby screws up his face with incredulity "Lovely Day? Not for us no. Our club has burnt down thanks."

"Indeedy do. My name is Sharp, Phil Sharp. Sharp by name, sharp by nature."

They stare at him in silence.

"Little joke of mine. Breaks the ice I find, bit of humour. What would life be if you can't have a laugh eh? I'm always laughing in this job."

The two stare at him in disbelief.

He grins at them, his eyeballs appearing huge through his glasses.

"Oh sorry. Regal and Royal. Here to have a look at your fire damage." He rummages in his duffle bag and produces his identity card "Now before I start, did you bring all the certificates and policies?"

Joby "Oh right. Nice to meet you Mr. Sharp. Yep, got them. All in order."

He hands the documents over "Do you want us to show you round?"

Mr. Sharp moves towards the makeshift door "No sir that won't be necessary. I'll just pop my hard hat on and get on with it."

He fishes a yellow hard hat out of his duffle bag and sits it on top of his woolly beanie. Delving again he produces a torch which he turns on and off a number of times.

Digger helps pull open the door "To be honest we have no idea how it started, a complete mystery."

Mr. Sharp blinks through his glasses as he clicks on his torch and enters the club" Don't worry sir, we'll soon find out the cause. Been doing this a long time. Nothing gets by me. Eyes like a hawk."

"Oh good, that's reassuring, isn't it Joby."

Joby grimaces and nods agreement "Oh yeah, very reassuring."

They walk a few paces away from the door to talk in private.

Digger starts panicking. "That's it we're stuffed. He looks like he knows what he's doing. We are proverbially as buggered as Barney's bull. Or as Pandora would say, gevuld."

Joby tries to be the calm one "Let's not panic yet. We know nothing, remember. I mean we truly know nothing and it's been our lucky week so far."

His optimism doesn't rub off on Digger "What's lucky about the club burning down. A lucky week for you maybe but I've invested a hundred grand and all I've got is a potential paternity suit. Oh, and a cough from smoke inhalation."

Joby's patience with Digger's whining was wearing thin. "Oh, stop moaning. If you'd cleaned the BBQ out like you should have, we wouldn't have been in this mess. Lazy sod."

Digger stands open mouthed "What happened to - We don't know what happened- all of a sudden?"

Joby waves a hand "You know what I mean. They have to prove what we already know. Don't panic, trust me."

Digger shoves his hands in his pockets as his shoulders slump "How many times in my life have I regretted you saying that."

*Trouble, trouble*
*And this misery*
*You're about to get the best of me*
*Someday darlin' someday darlin'*
*I won't be trouble, no more*

They find a patch of sunshine and station themselves in it, both staring at the door. For over twenty minutes they wait until Joby can't stand it any longer, so he advances slowly and pokes his head cautiously inside. Mr. Sharp is stood at the stage end of the club, holding up various charred objects and writing copious notes on his pad. His eyes, owl like one moment then screwed up like a mole the next as he looks at each object in close detail. Joby sidles back out.

Digger taps him on the shoulder "Well?"

"He's just looking at things."

"Is that good or bad?"

"How would I know? We'll find out soon enough."

Another five minutes and a slightly smudged, smokey assessor emerges from the gloom and gives the boys a grubby smile. They stand waiting for the verdict.

"All done. Very interesting, very interesting indeed."

He stands, slowly nodding his head. He jabs his thumb over his shoulder indicating back inside "Now that must have been quite a blaze. Phew, I bet that went up. Whoosh." He chuckles" Yep, that would have a beauty."

Joby hesitantly "I suppose so. We weren't here. We were asleep. At home."

"Quite" Mr. Sharp looks at his notes. "Well, I've had a good look around and I certainly have enough to make my report. But tell me, if I am not mistaken there seems to be the remains of a BBQ in there. I had a close look and again, if I am not mistaken, it's a BillyOh Collection 5 Burner Hooded Barbecue?"

Digger stammers "I can explain that. You'll laugh when I tell you."

Mr Sharp ignores him and continues regardless "I only mention it because I've got one myself. The wife and I love it. Brilliant piece of kit. No mess, none of that charcoal nonsense. Nice and clean. Turn it on, light the burners and off you go. Uses a lot of gas though that's the only problem. Ah well such a shame."

Joby hears the phrases "none of that charcoal nonsense." and "just light the burners." and turns to stare at Digger as Mr. Sharp proceeds.

"Pity it's ruined. They cost a fortune you know. When I saw it first, I thought, aha here's our culprit but the gas cylinder is still intact so obviously not. Must have been empty otherwise it would have gone up like bomb. There would have been nothing left to look at." More chuckling.

The boys answer in nodding unison "Obviously."

Joby feels a slight inkling of relief creeping into his bones as he dares to ask "So what do you think was the cause of the fire then?"

Mr. Sharp purses his lips "Well if pressed, my bet would be on an electrical fault behind the bar. Probably just above it in fact. Lots of signs. Was there was an electrical light fitting there, yes?"

Joby thinks "Yeah a small strip light under my uncle's picture."

"That's probably it then. Fault in there and that would have sparked a flame and with the alcohol optics so close there would have been a right blaze in no time."

Digger is in shock "So it was an accident?"

"Well, if you have all the builder's certificates showing the wiring was done to UK regulation BS 7671 and IEC 60446 standards then yes an accident."

Joby delves into the paperwork and pulls out a signed sheet "Yep we have all those."

"Well, these things happen I'm afraid. But it will all be in my report."

He takes off his hard hat and stashes it along with his torch in his duffle bag and makes ready to leave.

"Anyway, as I say I have enough information for now. We will be in touch as soon as we can. This is my card if you need any more information."

He hands a card to Joby who stares at it. Suddenly feeling confident he ventures "And when could we expect a settlement offer?"

Mr Sharp thinks for a second then peers through his glasses eyes wide "Well as soon as I do my report, then the wheels will kick into motion. I'll be as sharp as I can." He chuckles at his little joke "Sharp? Get it?"

Digger catches on "Oh yes, very droll, excellent."

Mr. Sharp holds his hand out "Anyway I don't see too many problems but it'll be up to the money people. You can start cleaning up now, so good luck and a good day to you both."

They shake hands and he marches off to the end of the street where his car is parked.

Digger is ebullient. "So, it wasn't me after all. It was an accident!" He does a little jig.

Joby slowly turns and stares at him. "Shut up you tart or I might just fucking punch you, right here, right now. Of course it was you. Don't be stupid. There was nothing wrong with that light!"

"But he said."

"I don't care what he said. You lit the gas and then stuck a ton of highgrade charcoal on a BBQ, that actually, according to an expert, apparently didn't need any. You build a furnace to rival Mount Etna then you drag it, molten lava and all, and dump it behind the bar."

He glares at Digger who is going red with embarrassment "Was the lid open at all? Why am I asking of course it fucking was! Oh, and where did you hang those tea towels…my guess over the lid."

He sees from Digger's expression he is right.

"So, the heat from the coals catches the tea towels alight, that causes a bottle of booze to explode and, luckily for us, it burns that bodged light fitting and the rest of the club. So don't say it wasn't you." He throws his arms in exasperation "Thank god the cylinder was empty and old hawkeye has the same BBQ. Even he wouldn't believe that anyone would be stupid enough to put charcoal on that BBQ!"

Silence reigns as they both take this in. Then Joby starts laughing realising the lunacy and luck in it all.

"Someone up there must really like us." He chortles out loud "They send us the only registered blind insurance assessor in Britain, with glasses like bottle bottoms and he has the same BBQ. I am never poo pooing Donna's karma theories again. I am turning Buddhist."He sees his pal is upset so he grabs him and gives him a little shake.

"Come on Digger cheer up, we got away with it. If they say it's an electrical fault then that's what it is. All you've got to do now is not be Safiya's long lost daddy and it's a clean sweep"

But Digger is inconsolable so Joby reminds him.

"Digger it's like I said yesterday, this is your freebie. And what a doozie it is, it's a cracker, makes my ruining a poxy merc look like child's play. Boy I can torment you with this for years" He looks to the skies. "Thank you, God. The future is bright, the future is taking the piss out of you!"

Digger lets out a small chuckle as Joby pulls the temporary door closed, locks it and puts his arm around his pal.

"Come on let's go. You can make me lunch. I fancy some beans on toast. Think you can manage that without burning it? On second thoughts let's not chance it, I'll do it."

Digger bursts out in relieved laughing.

*Now if your luck don't change,*
*boy don't you be sad*
*Yeah if your luck don't change,*
*now buddy don't you be sad*
*Now you really gotta learn Lord*
*take the good now with the bad*

# Chapter 16

Digger drives them back through the town. Joby checks his phone and realises he has three missed calls from Safiya. He calls her as they head home.

"Hi Safiya, sorry I missed you, we've been at the club - no with the insurance people - well they say it looks like an electrical fault - oh yeah very unfortunate - you've got the photo, excellent."

He glances at Digger driving alongside him and smirks, Digger grimaces.

"Well, we're heading back to my place now so why don't you pop up and we can have a look - ok then - see ya."

He puts his phone back in his pocket "She's on her way."

He looks at Digger's hangdog expression "Oh don't look so miserable, it won't be you. Probably."

They roll past the Parish Church, then the station and eventually reach Joby's house. He unlocks the front door and calls out.

"Donna, we're back."

No reply was the answer "Jolly good she's out, that's handy just in case."

Digger throws his coat over a chair "Just in case what?"

"You know, just in case your tadpoles did manage to permeate through the equivalent of the rubber Berlin wall all those years ago and you faint, or something."

"Ok stop it you're freaking me out now."

Joby laughs "Just joking. Let's have some lunch."

They adjourn to the kitchen where Digger sits at the table whilst Joby concocts beans on toast.

"Been quite a few days hasn't it Jobes."

"Certainly has, me old mucker, I will never moan about being bored again. Want sauce on this?"

"No thanks."

The front door bell ding dongs and they both stare at each other in a mixture of anticipation and trepidation. Joby slaps Digger on the shoulder and goes to let Safiya in. He opens the door and does some cheek kissing.

"Hi Safiya come on in. Go through to the kitchen, Digger's in there. Want some toast?"

"No thanks. Oh, while I remember, Rev Ness sends his condolences about the club. He says he'll say a prayer for you."

Joby trails behind her "Didn't do much good last time but thanks anyway."

She enters the kitchen "Hi Digger." She kisses him on the cheek "How are you? Bearing up? Strange old week, eh?"

Digger smiles a tight smile "Certainly has been. Let's hope it doesn't get any stranger."

Joby holds up the kettle "Tea Safiya?"

"No, nothing thanks." She rummages in her bag as Joby and Digger wait uneasily. "I brought that photo for you to look at. My aunty wrote a little note with it. She seems to remember my father being in property or something like that."

They stare at her.

"She seems very certain that this man is definitely my father. No doubts she says. Ah here it is."

She hands a small colour photograph to Joby who stares at it for a full minute. Staring back at him is the very beautiful image, from years gone by, of the stunning Myra and next to her, his arm around her shoulders a good looking man in a white shirt, tie and a smart, expensive suit.

Joby stares on. He knows the suit is expensive because it's his suit, dark blue with a slight red stripe. The man's hair is sleekly combed back. Smooth. Joby stares intently at the face and sees it smiling back, the same way that he had seen it thousands of times before. He can see Safiya in the mix of the two, clear as crystal. His hand shaking, he eventually hands the picture to Digger.

Safiya looks intently at Joby "Are you ok? Do you know him, do you know my dad?"

Digger looks at the picture a huge grim spreading across his face. The weight dropping from his shoulders.

"Bloody hell. Know him. Oh yes, we know him angel. Joby knows him really well. Joby why don't you tell Safiya who her Dad is or shall I do the honours."

Joby explodes and throws his arms in the air and stomps about the kitchen.

"Un-fucking-believable! The cheating, conniving, long haired, dog dicked, sheep shagging bastard. Not only did he steal our wheeze about estate agents he even borrowed my best suit. I loved that suit! Oh yes I know him Safiya." He paces around the kitchen muttering and grumbling.

Pointing agitatedly at the picture Joby rants on "He called us spivs! Men in suits are spivs that's what he used to say. If I - if I could get my hands on him, I'd strangle him!"

Safiya is wide eyed at Jobys rantings "Who is it?"

"Who is it? Who is it? I'll tell you who it is. The laziest, sneakiest .... The one person who has caused me more grief than any other person in this world. Who is it? It's Ken! Probably the only time in his life he ever wore a suit or combed his hair. He had his wicked way then buggered off gigging somewhere."

Safiya shrieks "Your Uncle Ken is my father. Oh, Joby that's wonderful."

She claps her hands in joy but then the tearful realisation strikes her. "But he's dead and now I'll never get to know him. Oh, Joby"

Unfortunately, her disappointment is wasted on Joby who fumes on.

"Better off that way angel please believe me. If he wasn't already dead, I'd bleeding kill him."

Joby paces some more. Digger tries to help in his own way. Rubbing his hands together "So Joby that means that Safiya is your cousin then."

Joby stops pacing and glowers at him "Thanks for that Digger."

Safiya wipes a tear and jumps up and joyfully hugs Joby nearly knocking him and the kitchen chairs over.

"It's wonderful news. I'd only seen that picture of Ken over the bar before and you couldn't see anything of his face on that. All hair and bits."

"Indeed angel. It's the bits that caused all this trouble."

Joby wriggles free and drops into a chair.

He lets out a big sigh "Don't get me wrong I am <u>really</u> delighted that we found your Dad, but it's a shock. Let me think a second. Donna said you looked familiar, how right she was."

Safiya beams "So you are my cousin and Donna is my - cousin in law." She turns "And Digger is…"

Joby interrupts "A complete arse, yes we all know that. Sit down Safiya we need to talk."

She sits excitedly opposite Joby on the edge of the kitchen chair. Digger is leaning against the wall beaming from ear to ear.

Joby composes himself and attempts to unravel the situation.

"Let me think. Safiya, if Ken is your Dad and yes, now I can see a likeness, then yes, I am indeed your cousin. But more important than that, you are Ken's closest relative not me. So, in reality everything in his will should have gone to you, not me. You see?"

Safiya clasps her hands to her face and gasps "No Joby don't say that. I don't want anything. Just finding him and you, is enough."

"That's very nice Safiya but I was brought up to face my responsibilities."

Digger snorts "Ha! That's a laugh."

Joby ignores him "There also is the small matter of Ken's guitar."

Safiya frowns "That old guitar?"

Joby relates the previous afternoon's revelations to her. Digger, as only a true friend can be, is delighted at Joby's discomfort and nods like a grinning Cheshire cat as the true extent of the estate is revealed.

Safiya listens wide-eyed "But Joby he left it to you just like he left the lockup and the money to you. He loved you. He didn't know I existed. You and Digger built that club and I certainly wouldn't want to take that from you. It's yours and Digger's."

She thinks a bit more and adds "And anyway I don't want to be saddled working behind that bar all my life. As much as I love you all. Mickey and I want to travel."

Digger stops grinning "Mickey? You and Britney, travelling, together!"

Safiya smiles "Yes, me and Mickey. He's really nice you know. We want to travel. Must be in the genes I guess."

Joby is more interested in sorting his family tree out "That guitar is apparently worth a load and if we are certain that Ken is your father then I suppose, ethically, it's yours."

But before Safiya can reply they hear the front door opening and Donna and Pandora breeze in.

Joby wanly smiles at his wife as she surveys the scene. "Hi Donna. Safiya has that photo of her Dad and guess what?"

Pandora breaks in "Don't tell me, it's you, you shag hond. I knew it all along. I told you Digger!"

"No, it's not me you Dutch tart. It's Ken."

A stunned silence falls over the room for a few seconds until Donna breaks it.

"But that's wonderful Joby." She turns to Safiya "I said you looked familiar and now I see it, you're his image. Oh, come here." She hugs her "Welcome to the family."

"What?" Joby tries to explain over the wittering "Yes it's wonderful but don't you see the problems it throws up over the will. Safiya is his closest relative so I guess technically everything is hers."

Pandora puts her hands on her hips and shakes her head "Makes no difference Joby. A vill is a vill. I am sure old vots his face Villiams vill confirm that. It's up to you to decide who gets vot."

Donna "I think she's right Joby. Sorry Safiya but of course you could contest it."

Joby makes a snap decision "She most certainly won't have to contest anything. No need for any of that malarkey. Bloody waste of time and money. Anyway, I've made an executive decision."

Safiya looks surprised "You have?"

He takes her hand as he stands to make his pronouncement "Safiya, if Ken were here today, I know he would have been very proud to call you his daughter. Now, whether you'd have reciprocated is a totally different matter, cos he was a complete knob. However, he would have wanted me to do the right thing for you and the right thing is that we share whatever proceeds come from that bloody guitar. There will be enough for us both."

Donna smiles proudly at her husband "Perfect Joby. Well done my little man." She turns to Digger for support "Great eh Digger?"

Digger shrugs and sighs "Well to be honest, and if you really want my opinion....."

Joby sharply butts in "We don't! No offence but you can't even work a BBQ."

Safiya throws her arms around Joby's neck in a strangle hold "We have so much to catch up on. I have a new family, how wonderful."

Joby peers over her shoulder and nods to Digger "Go and make yourself useful and get us all a cup of tea please. Oh, and don't burn the water."

*We want to leave you happy*
*Dont want to leave you sad*
*We want to leave you happy*
*Dont want to leave you sad*
*Want to sing some blues*
*But dont want to sing them bad*

# Chapter 17

From that moment on, daily life became one whirling carousel of activity and change. Mr. Williams was as good as his word in finding a suitable outlet for shifting Ken's guitar. Without hesitation he went to the most famous auction house in the world Batterby's

On March 27th, 1752, Joseph Timpkins, founder of Batterby's, held the first-ever sale under his own name, the library of a certain Rt. Hon. Sir Phillip Standon, Bart. described as "containing several hundred scarce and valuable books." which sold for a few hundred pounds. Well over two centuries later, on December 4, 1986, Batterby's sold a single book, *The Writings of Philipe D'Lion*, for more than £6 million. Since those early days it's not just prices that have grown considerably but so too have the scope and scale of Batterby's itself. John Timpkins would hardly recognize his old firm were he to take a stroll down London's present day New Bond Street. Certainly not this damp October Friday as it is Rock Memorabilia Day.

Joby leads the team up Conduit Street and around into New Bond Street. Mr. Williams is waiting in the understated entrance and leads them through the glass doors into the main auction room, already buzzing with anticipation of the morning ahead. They sit discreetly towards the back, barely able to contain their excitement. Safiya and Mickey have, with much hugging and kissing and various instructions, departed on their travels to the far east. They were despatched with an encouraging plea to enjoy themselves from Donna, Safiya's new surrogate mother, followed by an enlightening observation from Safiya's surrogate Dutch aunty that "Alle mannen zijn bastaarden and to overhandig op haar halfpenny." These were accompanied by a salutary warning from Joby (in his new role as guardian angel) that should anything happen to Safiya he would personally castrate Mickey, but for him to also enjoy his holiday. So, today it's the five of them fidgeting like kids waiting for Christmas morning to arrive.

Joby glances around the room. He had assumed that a rock auction would be full of rock stars and celebrities, and so, is somewhat disappointed just to see well dressed "spivs." and "spivettes" as Ken would call them. Not a codpiece in sight, all Paul Smith and Yohji Yamamoto.

The sale starts off with a variety of articles, some interesting some mind numbingly boring, that only a real collector would cherish. Though Pandora was tempted to bid on a pair of leather trousers once worn by Freddy Mercury but decided they would be too tight even for her.

The auction rolls on. And then it is time. The room goes quiet as the auctioneer consults his catalogue and pronounces "Lot 187. A 1964 Red, Fender Stratocaster guitar owned, played and subsequently burnt onstage in 1965 by Jimi Hendrix. Full provenance accompanies this item and it is a totally unique, and exceptional example, as it is the first known instance of him burning a guitar. A rare and exciting piece."

A low rumble of mumbling fills the room.

"As well as those of you present here, we have twelve phone and internet bidders. The bidding will be in pounds sterling so without any more delay I will start at one hundred thousand pounds."

A hand goes up and with it so does the price.

Fidgeting no more, Digger and Joby sit stunned as the price leaps in twenty thousand pound increments. Within a minute it is at three hundred and ten thousand pounds. The bidders drop out or ring off one by one until only two are left. Both on the phone and both in the USA. The auctioneer looks to the bidder's representatives at either the side of the room.

"Three hundred and ten thousand. Do I hear Three hundred and fifty thousand pounds?" He asks, looks and waits

Under his breath Digger mutters "For fucks sake hurry up." Joby stares.

Quiet instructions are received from across the pond. The auctioneer quietly confirms the instructions and makes the announcement.

"Two million pounds"

Confusion breaks out in the room. The auctioneer vainly tries to get silence but the noise continues as he seeks further clarification.

"Can you please confirm that bid. Two million pounds?"

A nod from the side of the room.

Joby is stunned "What did he say? Did he say what I thought he said?"

But before anyone can answer him across the room the rival telephone bidder issues their instructions.

"Two million five hundred thousand pounds"

Joby erupts "What?"

More bedlam.

"Please ladies and gentleman can we have silence. Please!"

Slowly the noise subsides. Joby and his team sit in quiet amazement at the developments not knowing if this is real or some joke.

"The current bid stands at two million five hundred thousand pounds and is against you sir."

Expectancy now fills the room. More talking into phones then a nod and "Three million."

More hushed conversations then a shake of the head.

"The bid then stands at three million pounds. Giving full warning, I will sell."

He looks left, he looks right. The room holds it's breath waiting, but suddenly the gavel drops with a subdued tap.

"Sold to our Los Angeles phone bidder for three million pounds. Congratulations."

As the gavel goes down, massive applause goes up.

Digger, Donna and Pandora are all beams as they grab hold of Joby. He simply sits there with a stunned look of bemusement and discomfort.

Donna is worried "What is it baby?"

"I think I've had a little accident in my pants Donna."

Reparations are done and the happy band are waiting in the reception area for Mr. Williams to complete the formalities. Nobody knew, or would say, who the buyer was except apparently, it was an American gentleman in Los Angeles who was determined to have the guitar. Although Joby was sad to see it go he managed to choke back the tears as Mr. Williams passed him the life changing piece of paper "There you are Joby, Ken's legacy to you."

Joby stares at it through blinking eyes "Thank you Mr. Williams. I guess he wasn't such a waster after all."

*Daddy, I need money, give it to your honey*
*Daddy, I need money now*
*All day long I hear that song*
*Oh, I'm pretty sure for that I go wrong*
*Fast as I can lend it, how you like to spend it*
*It just appears somehow*
*I've got the money, you've got champagne*
*If you don't stop spending, I'll go insane*

\* \* \*

The money is quickly transferred so that Donna and Joby can decide in their own time what to do with it. As promised half is immediately deposited in Safiya's account so that she can enjoy the fruits of her Father's dubious labours, if you could call winning a game of cards and conning a drummer out of a fortune, labour. The music in Joby's head is just rocking these days.

*I'll have no more crying no more lonely days*
*All my cares and worries will be far away*
*Whenever the sun shines when this whole day is through*
*And you'll be back tomorrow*
*That's why I've got the happy happy blues*

The next action on Joby's list was for to pay off the debt to Charlie, something he actually looked forward to doing, in a strange perverse way.

So early one morning Joby gingerly pushes open the workshop door and pokes his head in. He spies Charlie sat at his chaotic desk. He quietly picks his way between the cars and gingerly enters the cramped office.

Charlie doesn't even bother to look up "Waddya want?"

Joby places the cheque on Charlie's desk who picks it up and stares at it for some time before commenting.

"You owed thirty grand. This says thirty five."

Joby smiles "Look on it as interest accumulated and a special thank you, from me to you, for saving my club."

Charlie grunts, stuffs it into his oily top overall pocket and goes back to his work. "Well don't come banging on my door asking for it back when you're broke again."

Joby chuckles "Ok. It's a deal."

As there seemed to be nothing left to say, Joby makes his way out. As he reaches the street he stops and turns to see Charlie sat watching him over his glasses. He nods to Joby, a faint smile on his lips. Debt paid.

*I'm trouble in mind, baby you know that I'm blue,*
*but I won't be blue always*
*Yes, the sun gonna shine,*
*in my back door someday*

\* \* \*

As expected, the insurance company prevaricated over this and that for a couple of months but Pandora was on the case and worked her magic i.e tormented them constantly so that they eventually paid out the full insured amount.

Under John's management the restoration of the club was started and duly completed in record time. Restoration being the precise term, as the boys just wanted it back exactly as it was.

As Joby had said in the beginning "Stage there, bar over there, little kitchen area here. Burgers, scampi, soup in a basket and over there the bogs." It was all about the music really.

A replica of Ken's guitar resumed its pride of place in the newly refurbished gents and an even bigger picture of him graced the wall above the bar. A new sound system had been commissioned, but in all essence, it was as it had been, a basic blues bar for people to enjoy their music. The story of the guitar had given the club, and indeed Joby, an aura of celebrity and they had been on several real radio stations where amazingly Digger managed not to send anyone to sleep. No more was discovered about the mystery buyer apart from he was, seemingly, someone in the music business. As Mr. Williams had said, a mystery to pursue in the future, along with seeing what other gems, if any, Ken had stashed away. A new adventure.

So, once again it is the opening night at The Blues Hole and once more the club is a vibrant hive of talk, laughter and activity. A full house of friends old and new. Even Charlie and his surprisingly attractive wife are present. As Joby had said to Digger on seeing her "Well he's either filthy rich or has an enormous knob. Or both of course."

The evening's guests have been welcomed and are quaffing like there is no tomorrow, as Joby and Digger mount the stage, a sense of deja vu in the air.

They stand side by side, taking the applause. Joby steps up to the microphone

"Now where were we before we were so rudely interrupted?"

Mad cheers.

He continues "What can I say, it's been an interesting year but here we are again. Digger and I would once more like to welcome you all to the hottest club in the South, well it certainly was a few months ago believe me. Welcome to - The Blues Hole!"

More laughter and ironic cheering.

"As before, we can promise you the best in Blues and Soul and tonight for our re-opening, we have the wonderful Blues Hole Band with some very special guests."

"So, without further ado it gives me the greatest pleasure to say, Ladies and Gentlemen the Blues Hole Band!"

And so, it starts again. The place is rocking, the band playing like never before, people just having a good time. Joby quietly slips to the back of the club and proudly surveys the scene. He sees Digger mingling and laughing, Pandora serving drinks and flirting whilst admonishing "naughty boys," Donna, the earth mother gently making sure people are ok, and as he watches a warm glow permeates through his body. He thinks of the events of the past year. How he lost an uncle, found a beautiful cousin, kept his best friend, lost his sperm count, founded a church, opened a club, paid a debt and went from down to up to down and back to up again. He smiles at the thought of the fun and frolics. Up above his head proudly sits the picture of Ken, still in full groin thrusting action, looking down like some strange hairy icon: a constant reminder to Joby of the legacy of his past and a beacon pointing to a better future and, of course, the joys of constantly shooting for the moon.

Joby takes a moment to glance up at Ken and thinks to himself "After all this we could do with a holiday. I wonder what Vegas is like in the spring?"

*Out here the truth is all you can see*
*But there is a trick in the thick of it all*
*The ghost in a fog is a thin line*
*Between first light and last call*

*They say the sky is the limit*
*Reflected in the mirror of the mighty Mississippi*
*Shootin' for the moon*
*Crash landed in the Crescent City*
*Shootin' for the moon*

**The End?**

# Lyric Acknowledgements

Page 10 : Further on up the road written by Joe Medwich Veasey and Don D. Robey

Page 19 : Guitar Blues written by John Lees

Page 22 : Hard to Handle written by Otis Redding, Al Bell and Allen Jones

Page 35/235 : Shooting for the Moon written by Sonny Landreth

Page 41 : Lightning Bar Blues written by Arlo Guthrie

Page 48 : Runnin' Blue written by The Doors

Page 51 : Aint got nothing but the blues written by Duke Ellington and Don George

Page 55 : Invitation to the blues written by Tom Waits

Page 61 : Happy Blues written by William Squier

Page 67 : She gonna hurt somebody written by Wengell Mobley and Charles Elliott Wicks

Page 76 : If you wanna be happy written by Frank Guida and Joseph Royster

Page 80 : She Gonna hurt somebody written by Chuck Wicks

Page 88 : I'm Ready written by Muddy Waters

Page 93 : New York City written by Delbert McClinton

Page 94 : Roadhouse Blues written by The Doors

Page 95 : Miss You Blues written by Mark Knopfler

Page 105 : Nobody Knows you when you're down and out written by Jimmy Cox

Page 107/114 : Consequences written by Kevin Robert Hayes ,Bonnie M.Hayes and David Nagier

Page 121 : Someday After a While written by Freddie King and Sonny Thompson

Page 125 : There's Something on your Mind written by Cecil James McNeely

Page 127 : I'm Ready written by Willie Dixon

Page 130 : Show-Biz Blues written by J.J.Cale

Page 135: Police Station Blues written by Peetie Wheatstraw

Page 141/232 : Trouble in Mind written by Richard M. Jones

Page 148 : Blessing in Disguise written by Terry Taylor

Page 150 : Bath Water Blues written by Reverend Horton Heath

Page 155 : Unwed Fathers written by B.Braddock and John Prine

Page 162 : Jelly Jelly written by Gregg Allman

Page 164 : Don't Mess with Me written by Mick Moody and David Coverdale

Page 167 : Goin' Away Baby written by James A. Lane

Page 170 : I'm Gonna Burn Your Playhouse Down written by George Jones and Lester Blackwell

Page 172 : Late Blues written by T-Bone Walker

Page 182 : All You Ever Been Was Good written by Marvin Winans

Page 184: Even God Must Get The Blues written by John Scott Sherrill and Dean Anton

Page 187 : Somebody Pick Up My Pieces written by Willie Nelson

Page 193 : Rock Bottom Blues written by The Answer

Page 197 : Make it Feel Better written by Pat Bunch,Pam Tillis and Peter Wood

Page 201 : Just a Feeling written by Little Walter

Page 207 : Rich Man Blues written by Lucky Thompson and Mundell Lowe

Page 211 : Rosie's Restaurant written by Bobby Bare

Page 213: Trouble Blues written by Charles Mose Brown

Page 218 : Getting Older Every Day written by William Lee Conley Broonzy

Page 226 : Happy Blues written by Ella Fitzgerald

Page 231 : Money Blues written by Dave Leader, G.M.Coleman and Harry Eller

Page 231: Happy Blues written by Dale E. Noe and Billy Noe

Printed in Great Britain
by Amazon